The Ducal Detective

~A Novella~

Sarah E. Burr

Other books by Sarah E. Burr

A brief history…

Centuries ago, the corrupt and powerful priests of the Ancient Faith lorded over the continent. Poverty and sickness ravaged the world, forcing a faction of rebels to rise up and overthrow these tyrants preaching in the name of silent gods. The leaders of this movement, known in the annals of history as the Rebirth, proclaimed the realm would no longer answer to nameless demons and gods, but to the virtues of bravery, humility, kindness, and intelligence. Under these Virtues, the world would once again flourish. Sealing their pact, these newly anointed leaders drank the dew of the fabled kingsleaf flower, ensuring their offspring would be marked as the divine protectors of this new era with their royal eyes.

Welcome to the Realm of Virtues.

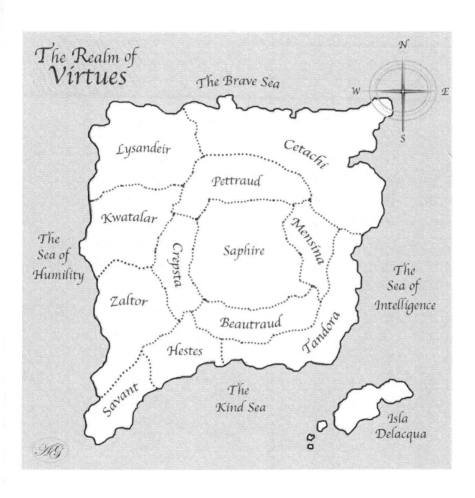

The Realm of
Virtues

The Brave Sea

N
W E
S

Lysandeir

Cetachi

Pettraud

Kwatalar

The
Sea of
Humility

Crepsta

Saphire

Mensina

The
Sea of
Intelligence

Zaltor

Beautraud

Tandora

Hestes

Savant

The
Kind Sea

Isla
Delacqua

Chapter One

A forlorn gaze from Arnie told her what she needed to know. Her request to delay the reception had not been granted. Her people were waiting for her to appear. She so desperately wanted to return to her rooms and toss the heavy crown off her head, but she knew a stunt like that would only fuel the rumors of her petulant immaturity. Tonight, she would stand before the gathered crowd and appease them with dancing and frivolity, when all she wished to do was mourn her mother and father. She thought it crass she had only been given a week to steel herself from her emotions, but she knew time was not on her side. She had to show the Realm of Virtues her nation was in capable hands, hands that did not tremble at the mere thought of her unwanted responsibilities.

Jacqueline Arienta Xavier, Duchess of Saphire, reached for the hand of her faithful lady-in-waiting. "Do you think they even considered postponing? For Virtue's sake, they only died a week ago!" Her words caught in her throat, still unable to fully comprehend her beloved parents were gone.

Lady Aranelda, her amber eyes full of sorrow in the candlelight, sighed and looked up at the brilliantly molded ceilings, gold and silver twinkling above them. "Jaquobie nearly laughed at the suggestion, I'm afraid to say."

The Duchess snorted at the mention of the High Courtier, a man who had been a constant thorn in her side since she learned how to walk. His barrage of manners and etiquette training had spoiled her childhood, and now, he was using the leverage of royal protocol to sweep her mourning under the rug. She often wondered if the man had any heart at all. "That doesn't surprise me in the least. Very well, let's get this horrific evening over with. I want all these people on their way home by dawn."

She gathered the skirts of her royal coronation ballgown. She never believed she'd be wearing it so soon. She had foolishly thought her father would retire of old age, handing her the throne after she'd had years to explore the realm and have adventures of her own. She'd only graduated from the Academy five years ago, and five years was not nearly enough time for her to have her fill of fun before her duties tied her down for life.

Lost in thought, she stroked the silky cream and gold fabric with her fingers, tracing a pattern through the diamond accents. She and her mother had refined the design of the dress over the years, always making some minor change as her tastes developed and matured. Years ago, the dress had been pink as candied sugar. The memory tugged a smile from her lips.

Arnie leaned in, placing a reassuring gloved hand on her shoulder. "Jax, I can tell Jaquobie you are not feeling well. You are the Duchess, now, after all. You can do what you want."

Jax looked up at her oldest friend, smiling at the familiar nickname. "Thank you, but you just said yourself, I am the Duchess now. It's not as simple as being able to do what I want anymore. I am a prisoner to the title."

Arnie rolled her eyes, not bothering to mask her fiery temper that often got both of them in trouble when they were younger. "A prisoner? Please, let's go look at the dungeons and see what being a prisoner really looks like."

"I don't mean to sound ungrateful for my lot in life. I know I am far better off than most people." Jax brushed a strand of shimmering caramel hair out of her face, tucking it back up under her crown. "It's just that I miss them so much. They were supposed to help me through all this when the time came." She felt her eyes mist over as visions of her parents swam before her.

Arnie bit her lip, as if sorry for chastising her dear friend. "I know you miss them, Poppy. We all do. They were truly great people."

Jax wrapped her trembling arms around Arnie's slender figure, pulling the woman close. "Please don't leave my side, Peach. I can't do this alone. Not today."

Arnie smiled at their pet names for one another, which had originally been bequeathed by their nannies growing up. Jax, for her favorite flower as a child, and Aranelda, for her favorite snack. "You've lost your mind if you even think I'd ever leave your side. I'll always be here for you, no matter what."

Giving her one last squeeze, Jax pushed back from Arnie and nodded in confidence. "I'm ready."

Together, they approached the royal guards posted at the ornate door at the end of the palace hallway. Jax heard the murmurs and speculations of her impatient guests from the other side of the door, the ballroom, no doubt, filled to the brim with noblemen and commoners alike, all anxious to see their new Duchess in the flesh. It had been a few years since she'd last attended a formal palace event. She wondered if any of her subjects would recognize the scrawny, awkward teen she'd once been underneath the regal woman she presented herself as now.

After she graduated from the Academy, Jax had convinced her father to let her study in neighboring kingdoms every summer, allowing her to advance her political prowess all while giving her time away from public scrutiny. She'd flourished into womanhood during this time, the unwanted spotlight no longer shining in her eyes everywhere she went. She'd spent her days in the world's most beautiful libraries, museums, and galleries, her mind open to all things new and exciting. She'd just started a tour of Hestes, one of the stunning southern provinces, with plans to learn about their rapidly expanding wine trade, when she'd received word about her parents' shocking demise.

"Your Grace," Arnie's familiar voice trumpeted an unfamiliar title, "we are all set."

Jax straightened her shoulders, her dazzling amethyst eyes locked on the doorway. This would be the first time in her entire life where she would be the only one in the Saphirian ballroom with amethyst eyes, the mark of one born into the ducal bloodline. In recent years, she'd always managed to find her father's gaze in the crowd, his tender expression a reassurance. Her mother, the eldest daughter of the Duke of Mensina, also bore the trademark royal eyes, although hers were tinged with the slightest bit of amber, evidence that her own mother, Duke Mensina's deceased wife, had been a high-born noblewoman. "I am ready," she repeated, more to herself than to those gathered around.

With a curt bow, the two royal officers pulled open the grand door, revealing the elaborately decorated ballroom. Gold and silver streamers cascaded from the domed ceiling, twinkling in the bright candlelight from gaudy candelabras placed strategically around the room by the palace staff. Purple irises, the royal flower of the Xavier family, stood at attention on every open surface not occupied by food and wine. The evening stars sparkled through the high arching windows, painting a fantastic scene before her. If Jax had not been completely heartbroken, the sight would have taken her breath away. But as her anger at being forced to attend such a lavish event was at an unprecedented high, she could not bring herself to marvel at the splendor. She simply floated in as she had been trained to do by Jaquobie and his cronies since childhood, waving demurely from the balcony to the vast array of citizens below. Their cries of jubilation and devotion fell on deaf ears. Overwhelming loneliness crushed her. If Arnie hadn't been beside her like a shadow, she might have very well turned around and run away. But her friend's calming presence eased Jax's breathing, and the Duchess maintained her composure as she descended the elegantly swooping staircase onto the dance floor.

Unsure what invisible force restrained her people from

swarming her, Jax made her way through throngs of whispering figures, each bowing low, not daring to meet her gaze. The path to her high-backed chair seated on top of the gilded platform was unobstructed, and within moments, she was perched overlooking the sophisticated chaos.

"Greetings, my beloved citizens," Jax purred whimsically, her mouth going stale at the flowery language. "I am honored to host this coronation celebration, just as I am honored to serve as your Duchess. I can only hope to fill half the shoes my father and mother left, and I hope you will join me by raising a glass to honor them this night." Like a puppet, she raised a sparkling glass of sweet wine to the stars, her stony expression set to fight back a torrent of emotion. She glared harshly at the crowd, prompting them to cease their curious whispers and join her in a moment of reflection.

"To her most Illustrious Highness, the Duchess of Saphire!" High Courtier Jaquobie's weasel-like squeal broke the silence, inviting people to repeat the devotion.

Jax found the man's dark amber eyes staring her down, filled with so much disapproval, they were almost black. She never understood how her loving and gentle father could tolerate his severe presence, let alone trust him with the education of his only child. Looking at him now sent a chill down her spine, tortuous memories of his lessons assaulting her thoughts. She dared not give him the satisfaction that he'd rattled her, so she merely looked away and nodded her head in thanks to the crowd for their affirmation.

"Please, enjoy the evening's festivities." With a wave of her hand, the music resumed from the string quintet in the back of the room. She sat down on her glowing, golden throne and watched as hundreds of partygoers began dancing and milling about once more. Arnie appeared behind her right shoulder, her face a mask of reverence.

"Shall I fetch you any refreshments, Your Grace?"

Jax rolled her eyes privately before smirking at her lady-in-waiting. "I'm fine for now, Lady Aranelda. Why don't you see if you can ascertain any new gossip from our friend, the Earl of Crepsta?"

To Jax's delight, Arnie's eyes brightened, and she bowed her head gratefully to the young sovereign. It was no secret Arnie and Earl Crepsta had mutual feelings for one another. The affair had blossomed long ago, during their time together at the Academy.

Watching her friend slink off to meet her beloved, Jax released a sigh. She hoped the Duke of Crepsta, one of her father's oldest allies, would soon request Arnie's hand in marriage on the Earl's behalf, as he happened to be the Duke's nephew. Arnie's marriageable eligibility had been elevated with her rise to the position of lady-in-waiting. If someone requested her hand before either Duke or Earl Crepsta made an offer, Jax would have a troublesome time—as sovereign—saying no without inciting ill will. As a friend, she of course wanted her dearest companion to marry for love, but both knew that their titles took precedence over their own feelings.

Jax watched Arnie sneak up behind Earl Crepsta, known by his friends as Hadrian, and tickle his side discreetly. His shock turned to obvious delight when he realized she was beside him. They made such a striking couple. Arnie, with her long chestnut hair, coppery skin, and near-gold amber eyes, was one of the most beautiful women in the room. Hadrian was imposingly tall, with sunflower blond hair, fair skin, and impressive muscles covering his athletic frame. His eyes, too, were a striking golden amber, for he was Duke Crepsta's nephew by marriage, not royal blood. Observing their tender embrace in all their beauty, Jax felt a stab of annoyance toward the Duke for not moving faster to secure the marriage and his nephew's happiness.

A bleak hole grew in Jax's already-shredded heart. When the match was finally made, it would mean she'd lose her closest friend and companion. The Earl would no doubt take his new bride back to his estate in Crepsta. The thought of Arnie not being beside her sent a flood of panic through her, but Jax could never ask her surrogate sister to give up true love for the sake of her duties as a lady-in-waiting. It was an unspoken vow between them. Once Arnie was married and living abroad, they'd continue to find ways back to each other, no matter what.

"Your Grace, shall I find you a dance partner for the next number?" High Courtier Jaquobie's steely voice infiltrated her daydreams. His long, pointy grey beard looked like a dagger, ready to slice through anyone who got in his way.

"No, thank you, Jaquobie." Jax left out his title, just to see him fume at her indignant tone. She was still upset that he had not even considered delaying the coronation to allow her time to mourn her parents' passing. "I'm not really in a dancing mood at the moment." She took a long drink of wine, savoring the taste.

Her flippant remark sparked fire behind his dark eyes. As a child, she was terrified of his nearly black gaze, but now, as a Duchess, it just fueled her ego.

"We are all very sorry about what happened to the Duke and Duchess, Your Grace." Jaquobie threw back his shoulders. "Please don't mistake our adherence to age-old traditions as indifference."

Jax stared the man down, surprised at the lack of malice in his voice, and more so, in his eyes. In all her anger and pain, she forgot her father had been like a brother to Jaquobie. The High Courtier was no doubt missing his dear friend. She was about to beg forgiveness for her rude remarks, when Jaquobie gave her a curt bow and turned on a heel, leaving her alone once more.

The night wore on in similar fashion. Most of her guests were too entranced by their own frivolity to speak with her directly, and when they did, the conversation was stilted and strained. Jax didn't know many of her own people well enough to speak with them conversationally. She and her father had bargained that once she turned thirty years old, she would return from her worldly studies and settle down in Saphire, becoming more familiar with her own people before she assumed the throne at age forty. It was tradition in the realm to hand down the throne once an heir reached a mature age, but the heir usually remained close to home their whole lives. She remembered her father's advisors in an uproar that their princess was to be sent away to explore the world, and now she knew why. She and her father had been foolish to think they had all the time in the world. She was practically a stranger in her own castle.

"Your Grace, perhaps it is time you retire?" Arnie's voice trickled into her ear, pulling her attention away from the empty wine bottle at her side.

Relieved her friend had returned, Jax nodded, pushing herself off the throne with restrained haste. "Yes, but let the ball continue on. Everyone seems to be enjoying themselves. It's hardly fair for me to ask them to end it just because I'm miserable." Jax tried to make her tone light and breezy, but her final words were biting.

Arnie tucked her arm under Jax's, tipping her head close to the Duchess's ear. "I think you'll find most are drowning their sorrows in alcohol. The mood out on the dance floor is very subdued. Your parents have not been forgotten," Arnie reassured her, stroking her gloved arm. "They were loved by all."

All the wine she'd been drinking to pass the time clouded Jax's vision, and her stomach growled, dangerously empty. "They're probably sad that they're stuck with a sovereign they hardly know, who made it well-known that she enjoyed being away from this stuffy place."

Arnie tutted beside her, leading her out one of the gilded doorways. "You were a child, Jax. Just give the people a chance to know the woman—the Duchess—you've become, and I'm sure they'll love you just as much as I do."

Jax couldn't help but let a few tears fall down her powdery

cheeks. "What did I do to ever deserve such a wonderful friend?" She leaned in and gave Arnie a sloppy hug, quite unbefitting of a royal. "Now, tell me, has Hadrian convinced his uncle to ask for your hand in marriage, yet?"

Arnie halted abruptly in the long, airy corridor, her face beet red. "I was hoping to have this conversation tomorrow."

Jax yelped with glee, clapping her hands like a toddler. "You simply must tell me what's going on. I demand it," she pompously requested, trying to summon her regal posture as the wine wreaked havoc on her senses.

Arnie tossed Jax a reproachful glare. "Absolutely not. How much did you have to drink tonight, anyway? You're knackered!"

An evening of drinking her sorrows away caught up with the Duchess, who sank to the carpeted ground, her gown fanning out all around her. "I...am...not!" She huffed in mock indignation before dissolving into a fit of laughter.

Sighing like a weary adult coaxing a devious child, Arnie motioned for two royal guards to help Jax to her feet and carry her to her private chambers. The walk through the castle, which normally would have taken ten minutes with all the stairs and winding hallways to traverse, dragged on, and Jax was in a drunken stupor by the time the guards arrived at the east wing doors.

"I'll take it from here, boys." Arnie sagged under the weight of Jax's slender body as she half-dragged her into the depths of the room. Not bothering to undress the Duchess in her current state, Arnie tenderly laid Jax out on her lavish four-poster bed, big enough for a family of five. "I'll leave some water by your bedside, Your Grace."

Even on the cusp of sleep, Jax could detect a slight bitterness in Arnie's words. "I'm sorry I'm such a bother, Peach. I just miss them so much." Clasping her hands sluggishly to her face, Jax dissolved into heart-wrenching sobs, the alcohol unleashing all her pent-up despair.

"You're not a bother. I just don't know what I can do to make it all better." Arnie brushed aside pieces of escaped hair, wiping tears and makeup off the Duchess's cheeks.

"Just don't leave me, at least not tonight." Jax grasped the woman's arms, pulling her close.

Curling up around her trembling body, Arnie clutched her dear friend, singing sweet whisperings until the Duchess was fast asleep.

Chapter Two

"Remind me never to drink Hestian wine ever again. My head feels like I've been crushed by horses." Rubbing her temples, Jax moaned as she rolled away from the sun's streaming rays assaulting her through the crack in her bedroom curtains.

"How about you remember to eat some food first, instead?" Arnie pulled her friend off the rumpled bedsheets, forcing Jax's aching body to attention. "If I had known you wouldn't be able to take care of yourself, I would have stayed glued by your side." Sounding slightly miffed and amused at the same time, Arnie motioned for the lady's maid, Uma, to enter the chamber and help Jax dress for the day. "I'll wait out in the sitting room."

Jax nodded, still feeling as though she were asleep underwater. Uma, a quiet, petite girl with mousy brown hair and the brown eyes of those who were common-born, deftly removed the coronation gown, stripping Jax down to her britches. A quick sponge bath ensued, as High Courtier Jaquobie had sent Arnie to inform her that Saphire would be receiving a delegation from the Duchy of Pettraud, leaving Jax no time to recover from the cruel effects of the wine.

"Uma, I'd like a bath drawn for me before bed tonight, if you will. Even if it is rude to leave my guests without a hostess." Jax knew this unexpected visit was not the girl's fault, but she failed to keep her dismay in check.

"Of course, Your Grace. I will have it ready at a moment's notice," Uma squeaked, busying herself with securing fresh undergarments. "I've prepared the Pettraudian blue gown for today."

"Seems fitting enough," Jax said as she stifled a yawn. "Although leave the corset off it this time. It makes me feel like I'm a collared dog." With that, Jax let her maid go to work. The gown was really quite lovely, made of the finest Pettraudian satin. It was more form-fitting than the designs she normally wore, but with her slender curves, it looked stunning. The periwinkle blue complimented her amethyst eyes, and as she appraised herself in the mirror, she admired the striking figure she presented. Joining Arnie in the private sitting room, she smirked. "Do I look like the disaster I feel inside my head?"

Arnie laughed. "If only we all could look as divine as you do with a hangover." She approached Jax with a plateful of tantalizing pastries. "I figured you might need some of this to sop up the wine in your stomach."

The Duchess lunged for a cherry popover, stuffing nearly the whole thing into her salivating mouth.

Chuckling, Arnie placed the tray on the tea table. "Ever the most elegant girl in the room."

Jax flopped down on a red and gold sofa, motioning Arnie to take one of the armchairs. "Uma, will you come get us once the delegation has arrived. I don't want Jaquobie being the first one to greet them."

"As you wish, Your Grace." Uma curtsied, taking her cue to exit the room, leaving the two women alone.

"So, before I rudely disintegrated last night, you were about to tell me about you and Hadrian." Jax dove right back into their conversation, grabbing another popover.

Arnie's face flushed at the mention of Hadrian's name. "It might be best to wait until after you've received the delegation. Jaquobie says this visit is extremely important. A test, if you will, of your endurance."

"Forget Jaquobie. If you don't tell me now, I'll be so distracted for the rest of the day, I'll likely start a war between us and

Pettraud." Jax waved a hand at Arnie's concerns, continuing to munch her way through the tray of pastries.

"Very well, then." Arnie sat up primly, wiping her dress nervously. "Hadrian did ask me when I thought it would be the right time to get engaged. He wanted to know if I'm able to leave Saphire, after only just becoming your lady-in-waiting."

Although she kept her face neutral, Jax stiffened at the thought of Arnie leaving her side.

If she sensed the growing tension, Arnie ignored it and continued. "I told him that while it would be a dream to become his wife, there is no way I could possibly vacate my post now. I told him that I would like to stay here at least a few more months."

"A few more months?" Jax exclaimed, her shock overshadowing her concern. "Peach, you know I love you more than anything and never want you to go, but making that man wait a few months might spell disaster! What if his uncle makes him marry someone else? What if someone else asks for your hand? If it's advantageous for Saphire, you know I wouldn't be able to say no."

Arnie smiled, her face pale with remorse. "I know, and if any of those things were to happen, I would accept it. It is not in the best interest of the duchy that I abandoned it now."

"I hope you don't mean to abandoned *me* now." Jax's tone was cooler than she intended.

Arnie threw her hands up in sudden exasperation. "Well, of course, I mean you! What kind of friend would I be if I left the woman I love like a sister to figure this whole mess out on her own?" Jax was surprised to see tears in her friend's golden eyes. "I can't leave you now. And it's not because I feel obligated to stay and help. It's because I love you, and I loved your parents as if they were my own, and I don't want to leave."

Jax dropped her pastry and rushed over to Arnie, scooping her up in her arms. "You know that I want you by my side for as long as you will have me. I just don't want you throwing away your own happiness because of me. I will be all right. I will, I promise."

"I know you will be. And as much as I care for Hadrian, right now, my place is with you," Arnie whispered into Jax's shoulder, burying her face into the Duchess's gleaming hair.

Pulling away from the embrace, a thought popped into Jax's mind. "Did Hadrian leave this morning?"

Arnie nodded. "He left at the top of the hour. Why?"

Jax paced the length of the room. "Send him a message, inviting him to be our guest next week. I have an idea."

Arnie shot her a questioning look, but Jax mimed sewing her lips shut. "All in due time."

Arnie's requests for more information were interrupted by Uma's reappearance. "The delegation has been spotted, Your Grace. Jaquobie is in a meeting with the junior courtiers, so he has not been alerted of Pettraud's arrival."

"Excellent, Uma. Thank you. Please make sure the throne room is in order, whilst I receive our guests in the courtyard." Jax hurried across the sitting room, shaking her dress free of breadcrumbs. "Lady Aranelda, you will join me once you have sent a formal invitation to Earl Crepsta."

Arnie bowed her head in understanding and left the chamber with Uma, giving Jax a rare minute alone to compose herself. She knew nothing about who traveled with the Pettraud delegation. Jaquobie had only just received word from a royal page this morning that the representatives planned to stop on their way home from a tournament in neighboring Mensina to pay their respects.

It surprised Jax that Mensina had not postponed the grand knights' tourney. Her mother had once been the heir to its throne, after all. Bitterly, Jax reflected that her grandfather had never been one to let love and emotion get the better of him. The more she thought about it, her mother, too, would have been mortified if tradition was uprooted over something as "trivial" as her death. Amaryllis Mensina always put duty before her own needs. It was the royal way of things.

Surveying her figure one last time in the mirror, Jax made sure her crown sat securely in her hair before leaving her chambers. She marched with purpose to the enormous courtyard, taking her place at the top of the steps to await her guests. The gardens looked impeccable in the late morning light, a cacophony of flowers blooming everywhere. She stood proudly, knowing her castle did not look the least bit affected by death. If anything, the warm spring air made it appear more vigorous than ever.

A horn trumpeted in the distance, signaling the Pettraudian delegation's arrival at the lower gates of the palace. Perched at the top of a small mountain, her pristine home overlooked the city of Sephretta, the capital of the duchy. The sprawling valley was full of bustling markets and busy banks, for Sephretta was the wealthiest city in the realm. Her father's strong trade agreements over the past decade had caused the economy to boom, something Jax was particularly proud of because she had been instrumental in making it happen. If anything, her time abroad had trained her in the art of negotiation, and she'd often put her skills to the test arranging these contracts on behalf of her father.

She waited, soaking in the sun, as the delegation lazily made its way to the gates of the courtyard. They obviously did not expect the Duchess herself to greet them, for she noticed the group scramble to attention as they entered through the gardens. "Your Grace, we humbly ask your apology if we have made you wait." A pudgy man, likely a courtier, came to the front of the column and bowed lowly, his face red with embarrassment.

"No apologies necessary. The sun's rays treated me nicely, especially after being cooped up yesterday due to the coronation activities." The Duchess smiled at the man, hoping to relieve him of unneeded stress.

"Thank you, Your Grace. On behalf of the Duchy of Pettraud, I extend our greatest sympathies for your loss. Your parents were good friends of the Duke and his late wife." The man straightened, regaining his composure.

Jax nodded, hesitant as to how to address the man speaking to her. "I hope to continue that friendship, Sir...?"

"Oh goodness, how silly of me. I am Courtier Rence, Your Grace. I serve under the High Courtier of Pettraud."

"Welcome to Saphire, Courtier Rence. I understand you are traveling home from the Mensina tourney?" Jax surveyed the rest of the group, made up of polished knights. Rence seemed to be the lone statesmen among them.

"Yes, Your Grace. The Knights of Pettraud performed well. Several of our men took home a trophy or two." Rence wiped sweat from his balding head, growing crimson under the light of the sun.

"Then we shall have a celebratory feast to honor their greatness." Jax looked over the knights assembled, knowing that her own guards were watching from hidden spots all around the courtyard. "Please, do come inside and recover from your journey."

"That would be most excellent, Your Grace," Rence sputtered, looking back through the gate. "We are still waiting for one more in our party to arrive."

As if on cue, a well-crafted carriage rolled through the entryway, pulled by two blindingly white horses. Jax stiffened, wondering who would be traveling in such lavish style on the way home from a knight's tournament.

"If I may, Your Grace, introduce Lord Percival Pettraud." Courtier Rence made a sweeping bow, this time to his knees, as the carriage door swung open and a figure emerged.

Jax sucked in her breath, taking in the form approaching her. Lord Pettraud was dashingly tall, his pale lavender eyes glittering in the sun. His ceremonial tunic clung to his strong chest, his arm muscles rippling underneath the expensive fabric. Pushing his dark, curly hair away from his face, he smiled and bent at the waist before the Duchess.

"Greetings, Your Grace. I have heard tales of your beauty from my brothers, but I have never had the fortune to gaze upon one so fair. Their words did not do you justice." His voice was a soothing baritone, sending shivers down her spine.

Hoping her Duchess-of-Saphire mask was well in place, Jax extended her hand for a kiss. Lord Pettraud took it tenderly in his own, bringing her fingertips to his lips with almost eye-rolling swagger.

"I am pleased to welcome you to my home, Lord Pettraud. Do come inside." Jax turned on her heel and led the party into the grand hall.

"Forgive my surprise at being greeted by the Duchess, Your Grace. We did not expect to see you up and about the castle." Lord Pettraud, rather imprudently, walked directly beside her.

Jax turned her gaze toward his, raising her eyebrows. "And why did not you expect to see me in my own home?"

Lord Pettraud's cheeks suddenly reddened, as if knowing he'd made a fatal error. "I simply meant…well…with the death of your parents, we did not expect you to be in the state of mind to receive visitors."

Knowing he was coming from a place of concern, Jax replied with a light tone. "I believe your father received my father's delegation the day after his dear brother passed away. I do not remember my father being surprised to see Duke Pettraud up and about." She spoke curtly, internally repelled by the double standard.

Lord Pettraud's face flushed even more. "I did not mean to suggest anything, Your Grace."

She smiled tightly. "While my parents' passing was a devastating blow, please do not assume that I am weak and at the mercy of my emotions."

Lord Pettraud shook his head, clearly overwhelmed with the direction their conversation had taken. "Of course not, Your Grace." He fell silent as she continued to lead them towards the open doors of the throne room.

"Please," he suddenly sputtered. "I have completely made a fool of myself and my father. Could you perhaps give me a chance to reintroduce myself?"

Not immediately answering, Jax strode to her political throne, different than the one she had sat on last night. Her political throne, whilst still made from gold, was much simpler in design, yet still imposing in its size and elegance.

"Your Grace?" Lord Pettraud asked again.

"Is this your first royal delegation, Lord Pettraud?" Jax responded, draping one arm across an armrest.

At this question, Lord Pettraud's face broke out into a sheepish grin. "Is it that obvious?"

His boyish candor made her chuckle. "Just a bit, I'm afraid."

The other knights and Courtier Rence shuffled into the throne room, standing a respectable distance to allow the two to continue speaking in private.

Looking back at his men, Lord Pettraud seemed to shake his head at the absurdity of the moment. "I'm the brawn, not the brains, one might say. My father thought it was time I assume some responsibilities other than jousting for the entertainment of the kingdom, as I couldn't possibly mess up a congratulatory visit regarding your new title. But who wants to offer congratulations to a person who's just lost their family?"

Jax wasn't sure if he was talking to himself or to her, so she didn't reply. She appreciated him sharing his opinion at his father's rather callous request. She certainly did not feel like being congratulated.

Turning back to make eye contact, Lord Pettraud bowed again. "I'd like to reintroduce myself, Your Grace. While I am the seventh son of Duke Pettraud, I am known to my friends as Perry. I hope you will come to think of me as a friend."

At the sincerity in his lavender eyes, her frigid attitude began to thaw. "Welcome, Sir Perry. I am Jacqueline Arienta Xavier, Duchess of Saphire, but my friends call me Jax." She winked at him, their shared connection quickly taking root. She admired the young man's humble nature and the ability to admit he was wrong.

"Jax." Perry simply confirmed with a nod, motioning to Courtier Rence to join them. The courtier puffed out his chest, readying himself for an audience with the Duchess. "I'll let this man speak on behalf of my homeland, for fear I might misspeak and cause a war between our nations. Besides, he's the one who receives all my father's missives, not me."

Jax laughed, thinking about the similar comment she'd made to Arnie earlier that morning. "Please, before we focus on matters of state, let us all have some refreshments."

The palace staff appeared from the shadows bearing water, juices, fruits, and cheese. The worn-out knights eagerly drank and stuffed their faces with the goods. Jax tried to restrain herself, but cheese had always been her downfall, especially when fighting the remnants of a hangover. She demurely nibbled on bits of smoked gouda and had a sneaking suspicion that only Perry detected just how many pieces she'd hidden in the folds of her skirts.

Amidst the refreshments, Arnie appeared by Jax's side, taking in the scene. She nudged Jax impishly, nodding her head in the direction of Lord Pettraud, her eyebrows raised suggestively. Just because she was in love with Hadrian, didn't mean Arnie couldn't enjoy the sight of other attractive men.

"He is quite gorgeous, isn't he?" her lady-in-waiting mumbled from the corner of her mouth.

Jax giggled, quickly filling her in on Perry's disastrous first impression. "But I will give him credit for owning his behavior entirely. I can only imagine the horror Jaquobie would have expressed if he had been present."

"As I indeed should have." From out of nowhere, the High Courtier appeared at her other side, his face a mask of displeasure. "Why was I not informed of the delegation's arrival?"

"Because I am perfectly capable of greeting my guests on my own," Jax said through gritted teeth. "Don't worry, I have not forgotten the endless lessons you have burned into my memory on how to behave like a lady."

Courtier Rence approached her throne before Jaquobie could snap a retort. "This must be the legendary High Courtier of Saphire. I am honored to meet you, sir." Rence reached out a hand for an eager shake.

Rolling her eyes discreetly while Jaquobie greeted his fan, Jax turned to Arnie. "Legendary? There will be no living with him now."

Arnie tried to hide a snort as the two courtiers turned their attention back to Jax.

"I was just telling High Courtier Jaquobie how hospitable you have been with all you have going on, Your Grace."

Jax gave Jaquobie a triumphant "I told you so" smirk, before turning back to Rence. "I suppose for the first time, I truly understand how big a palace this is. It's nice to fill it with visitors, Courtier Rence. I hope we have the pleasure of your company for at least a night?"

Rence looked very pleased by the offer. "Your Grace, we would be delighted. I am sure our knights would appreciate a warm bed. Forest floors are no longer as inviting as they once were to this old man." He gesticulated to himself. "Are you sure it is not an imposition?"

Thinking back to last night's ball and the longing to be alone with her grief, Jax put on her most charming façade. "Of course not. Pettraudians are forever welcome in our halls. Please, stay as long as you like."

"A generous invite, Your Grace. Thank you." Rence bowed once again.

"Aranelda, would you please escort the delegation to the west wing and show them their rooms? I'd like to suggest our guests rest for the afternoon and recover from their long journey from Mensina. In the meantime, I will have a glorious feast arranged so that we can converse over a full table," Jax announced. She sensed Rence's dismay that whatever he had to say to her must wait a little while longer.

Not giving him the chance to protest, Jax took her leave of the throne room, handing the reins over to Arnie to deal with the horde of men. She decided she wanted Uma to draw that bath now.

Chapter Three

A feverish knock on her apartment doors startled Jax from a daydream, the water sloshing around her. It was barely lukewarm now, her skin pruned from sitting in the bath for much longer than she intended. Rising from the large basin and grabbing a towel, Jax's brow wrinkled in annoyance for a moment before remembering she'd dismissed Uma for the afternoon to ensure her time alone.

The knocking continued, forcing Jax to hastily throw on a dressing gown before racing for the door. Whoever had the audacity to bother her like this better have an important reason.

Her mood plummeted as she opened the door, her wet hair sticking to her face. "Master Vyanti? What in the Virtues are you doing here?

At her choice of language, the elderly man's face twitched. Master Vyanti was her father's court physician, but to many, he was much more than that. In his prime, he had been a shaman — a priest — of the Ancient Faith, an archaic religion believing in gods and demons subdued long ago by a revolution led by the Children of the Virtues. Instead of gods, enlightened people prayed to the Virtues of kindness, humility, bravery, and intelligence.

Despite their oppressive leaders being overthrown hundreds of years ago, the Ancient Faith lingered on, still causing tension in certain areas of the realm. Jax's father, not wanting further unrest in his duchy, had appointed Master Vyanti as court physician as a peace offering, a symbol that the Ancient Faith and the Virtues could live in harmony. Jax, having grown up as a Child of the Virtues, still struggled to understand the old man's way of life, and often inadvertently offended his religion with her off-the-cuff remarks.

Vyanti disregarded her exclamation and pushed into her room, uninvited. "I am sorry to barge in on you like this, child, but I have a grave matter to discuss with you."

Seeing the obvious distress on his face, Jax clasped her dressing gown tightly and ushered the man into the sitting room. "I've never seen you this rattled, Master. What is it?"

Vyanti leaned back in one of the armchairs, looking like he was steeling himself for what was to come next. His robes were stained with dark blotches, his wiry grey hair a mess, and the smell clinging to his clothes almost made her gag. Glancing up at her with wild eyes, his chin trembled. "I have just come from examining your parents."

Jax's stomach dropped. "What?" She realized the stains on his robes were from blood. Her parents' blood. Shaking in anger, she yelled. "Why couldn't you just leave them in peace?" She cursed the Ancient Faith, for it had a vulgar ritual that involved removing the organs of the dead and burning them, allowing their spirits to join their silent gods. Where her father supported the Ancient Faith, Vyanti must have thought the Duke's body was subject to this archaic ceremony.

Shaking his head adamantly, Vyanti held up his hands. "No, no, no, Your Grace. It is not what you think. Only those true to the Ancient Faith are cremated in such a way. I was merely examining their bodies for scientific purposes."

Jax put her head in her hands, releasing her relief that her parents had not been touched by the Ancient Faith's customs. They would be interred in the ducal cemetery, entirely whole in mind and in body, like all her ancestors before her. "Go on."

Master Vyanti clasped his hands. "I was preparing their bodies for internment, and I couldn't help but notice that they did not reflect any signs of trauma. In fact, I could not find a single indicator that they died from their carriage crashing. No broken bones, no bruises…nothing."

Trying to bury the images of her parents' bodies strewn across the debris of their broken carriage, Jax looked at Master Vyanti in confusion. "What are you saying?"

He leaned in close, the smell of death wafting from him. "Your parents were dead before the carriage overturned."

Her blood ran cold.

"I came here to request permission to perform an autopsy so I can determine what actually killed them."

Fighting through the shock of what she had just heard, she assessed the physician. "Have you told anyone else about this?"

He looked offended by her question. "Of course not, Your Grace. I prepared the bodies alone, and I came directly to you with my findings."

Jax bit her lip, planning her next move. "You have my permission to perform the autopsy, on one condition. I will be there beside you. Please wait here while I change into something more appropriate."

Silencing his protests with a formidable glare, Jax rushed into her bedroom and buttoned herself into a simple dress before hurrying back to an awaiting Vyanti. "We must be quick about this. I don't want anyone catching sight of me and asking questions we don't have the answer to."

With a slight nod, Master Vyanti led the way to the infirmary. Although, instead of entering the hospital wing on the main floor of the castle, they descended deeper into the recesses of the palace, near the catacombs. When Jax realized they were approaching the burial preparations room, a chill jolted down her spine. She had never been here, mostly because she had been too young when her grandfather passed away, and up until seven days ago, a member of the royal family had not needed burying. Even though it had been offered by Master Vyanti earlier in the week, Jax had not had the heart to visit the bodies of her parents.

The pair entered the preparation room in deafening silence, each too absorbed in their thoughts to converse with one another. Master Vyanti lit the lanterns dangling from the arched ceiling, illuminating covered examination tables in the middle of the morbid space.

Jax's stomach seized as she took in the haunting shape of a lifeless body beneath one of the filmy sheets. The size and shape suggested her father lay underneath. She closed her eyes, not ready to see the handsome, charismatic man succumb to death. She listened as she heard the swish of the sheet, the prodding and poking of stiff skin and muscle. It nearly made her vomit, Vyanti's quickening breathing the only life-like noise in the room.

A small pop resonated in her hot ears, followed by a gasp.

"Your Grace. If you will please look at this, we have our answer."

Jax didn't know how she summoned the courage, but she inched open her amethyst eyes, narrowing immediately toward the direction of Vyanti's pointed finger. It took her brain a moment to catch up with what her eyes were seeing. Her father's lightly lined face, the paleness of death fighting against his tanned cheeks and winning, his eyes closed, as if he were sleeping. His face was perfect. She'd had nightmares of his mangled body, bruised and bloodied from the crash, waiting underneath the cart to die. But his face was unmarred. No bruises, not even a shaving nick. He was perfect. Except for his mouth. The pop must have been Vyanti opening the Duke's mouth, his jawbone moaning in protest. She assessed his pearly white teeth, his smooth lips. They were flawless. It was his tongue that made her stomach reel. His tongue was gangrene, rotting and molding from within his untarnished head.

"May the gods protect us," Master Vyanti mumbled, frantically waving his arms around in some type of devotion. He turned to meet her perplexed gaze. "Your Grace, the Duke was poisoned."

Chapter Four

His words echoed throughout the quiet chamber. Poisoned? That could only mean…

"Someone intentionally did this to my father. He was murdered," Jax seethed, her anger and rage surpassing her grief. Someone had deliberately robbed her of this great man. Looking into Master Vyanti's wide eyes, she snapped, "Examine my mother, as well." Her attention flickered to the second covered figure in the cavernous space. A powerful resolve flooded through her. "I want it confirmed."

Master Vyanti quickly went to work while Jax turned her gaze skyward. The thought that her father had an enemy dangerous enough to kill him truly terrified her. For so long, she'd lived in blissful oblivion that her father was the most beloved ruler throughout all the duchies. He'd negotiated for peace, human rights, and prosperity for not only his own people, but for all in the realm. Why would someone want to end his life?

"Your Grace, the Duchess suffered the same fate, I'm afraid." Master Vyanti's report was delivered with a grim expression.

It was almost as if she'd left her body and was looking down on the scene, watching herself, not as a daughter, but as a grand sovereign, pace around the room in a frenzy. She filed through her memories, all the knowledge she had accrued over the years, sifting out emotion and sentiment, focusing on logic and reason. "What time did my parents depart for their journey that morning, Vyanti?" She couldn't remember the details, having been in a state of shock when the Ducal Guard had relayed to her news of the accident.

Master Vyanti hung his head. "I am not sure, Your Grace. I, too, was away from the castle when they died, working with the brotherhood of physicians on a new antibody for the black fever."

Jax's lips tightened. If she could get confirmation that he was indeed at the symposium, she could officially eliminate Vyanti as a possible offender. Every other person in the palace remained a suspect. "I hope I can count on your discretion whilst I get to the bottom of this."

He looked rather shocked at her words. "Your Grace, wouldn't it be wise to hand this investigation over to the Ducal Guard? Captain Solomon can surely find the culprit responsible."

"The Ducal Guard failed to protect my mother and father," Jax scoffed. "In order for my parents to have been poisoned, someone must have tampered with their food...their drink...their clothes, even. That would mean there is a traitor in our midst. If we alert the Ducal Guard of this crime, we could scare our perpetrator away."

"Or prompt him to take action," the physician pointed out. "Your Grace, you are in danger. Either someone is out to end your bloodline, or they are planning on using you now that you are sovereign."

Jax contemplated his words. She couldn't deny the truth in both possibilities. "I'm not about to let anyone use me, Vyanti. I am quite stubborn, as I am sure you know," she commented dryly, and despite their surroundings, a wry smile flourished on the lips of the priest. She did not address the first scenario he'd mentioned. The death of her parents had brought her back home for a substantial time, the first in many years. Since she'd gone off to the Academy, she hadn't spent more than three or four days at a time in the palace. It was entirely possible she had been lured home and right into a trap. "Regardless, I don't think it wise to involve anyone in our suspicions, just yet. At this moment, the culprit thinks they have gotten away with murder. I'd like you to see if you can determine how they were poisoned and what was used. If we know the how we may be able to track down the who and the why."

"Yes, Your Grace." Master Vyanti bowed his head in acquiescence.

"Once you're done, continue with the burial preparations, as scheduled. We will still plan to entomb them at the private funeral..." Jax's voice trailed off and lightheadedness flooded her vision as reality sank in. "I've been down here for too long. If my maid returns, it will raise suspicion if I am not in my chambers. I also must see to my guests." With a sweep of her dress, Jax departed the catacombs and rushed quietly back to her rooms. The bathwater was still drawn, and although it had chilled significantly, Jax dumped a vial of lavender oil into the water and submerged herself in the tub once more. She shivered, but she doubted it was solely from the water's touch. Allowing her emotions out of their cage, the enormity of the situation overwhelmed her. The carriage crash was all a ruse. Someone had poisoned the Duke and Duchess and then went through a lot of trouble to elaborately stage their deaths. Had her parents been poisoned that morning? Was it their picnic lunch? Their water supply for the road? And their guards? All had been crushed by the carriage. Had they, too, been poisoned, or killed by those responsible for the plot?

Questions swirled around her mind as she took a scrub brush and set to work cleansing her skin and hair of the stench of death. She rubbed herself raw, drawing blood on patches of her arms and legs, unable to get the horrid smell out of her mind. Whoever did this to her family would pay dearly.

"Your Grace? Shall I help you prepare for dinner?" Uma's meek inquiry filtered into the washroom.

"Yes, Uma, I'm in here still." Jax quickly composed herself. Even timid Uma could somehow be involved with this treachery.

"Your Grace! You must be a shriveled old lady by now," Uma exclaimed as she flitted in through the doors. "I thought you would have dried yourself off hours ago."

"Yes, silly me, I just got lost in my thoughts," Jax said absently, rising from the basin as Uma wrapped her in a towel.

The efficient maid went to work on the Duchess's hair, twisting it up into an elegant bun. "This will hide the fact that it's still damp, Your Grace." Uma tutted, rushing to Jax's voluminous dressing room to find a gown for the evening. She settled on a dark blue number with silver trim, cutting an impressive figure and accenting Jax's eyes to the utmost.

After dabbing on some powder and rouge, Uma escorted Jax to the ceremonial dining hall, where she found Arnie waiting for her. Just seeing her friend made her want to dissolve into tears and tell her all about her torturous afternoon, but now was not the time. After they'd put their guests to bed, Jax would confide in Arnie, the one other person besides Vyanti she could trust. Arnie had been with her in Hestes when her parents died, after all.

Arnie must have noticed her sour mood, for she drew the Duchess close. "You look stunning. Lord Pettraud is going to lose his mind when he sees you."

Jax snorted at the thought. "What in the Virtues do you mean?"

Arnie leaned in, lowering her voice so the attending guards did not overhear. "I have a sneaking suspicion that this delegation has come to offer more than just its congratulations on your new title."

Jax's eyes popped open. "You can't be serious."

Arnie shrugged, suppressing giggles. "Let's just see what Courtier Rence has been dying to say all afternoon."

A new worry bloomed in her mind as Jax made her grand entrance into the regal dining room. She was in no mood to consider proposals of any sort, let alone ones of marriage.

Sitting down at the head of the lengthy, polished table, Jax motioned for her guests to do the same. Many of the knights were in ceremonial tunics, most likely leftover from their time at the tourney. Only Courtier Rence seemed to have been prepared to dine in a palace with his lavish robes.

Seated two people to her left was Lord Pettraud, looking unjustly handsome in his simple knight's costume. "Lord Pettraud," she commented, assuming formal language for the dinner, "did you and your party rest well?"

She caught him mid-sip, causing him to sputter into his wine. "Yes, Your Grace. Our accommodations are simply wonderful." He chuckled bashfully as he mopped up his wine-stained face.

"I must say, Your Grace, the palace of Saphire really has no rival." Rence spoke with reverence, pulling her attention away from Perry's sloppy manners.

Jax smiled at the courtier. What had this poor man done to deserve such an unwieldy charge? Perry hadn't even waited for her to raise her own glass. Doing so now, she signaled the rest of her guests to enjoy the Hestian wine she'd provided for the evening. Her own glass was filled with apple juice, still not having recovered fully from last night's drinking. "Please, enjoy our feast this evening. Saphire is always honored to entertain our dear friends to the north." She sipped her beverage austerely, watching everyone around the table do the same.

Once the food was served, conversations broke off amongst the group, leaving Jax to speak with those immediately around her: Arnie and Perry to her left, Rence and Jaquobie to her right. She had barely cut into her pheasant when Rence cleared his voice ominously.

"Your Grace, might now be the time to bring up business of state?" While his tone was courteous, she doubted he would accept no for an answer.

"Of course, Courtier Rence. What can Saphire do for Pettraud?" Jax placed her napkin down on the table, hiding her disappointment that the savory meal before her had been interrupted.

"While the circumstances of your ascension to the throne are heartbreaking, Pettraud is pleased to welcome such an intelligent and fair-minded ruler to the political arena, much like your father was," Rence began his speech deferentially. Jax couldn't help but infer that Duke Pettraud was relieved she wasn't a flighty wisp of a woman.

"I appreciate the Duke's faith in my ability to rule," Jax lamented. *Although I didn't ask for it.*

"But of course." Rence continued, "The Xavier bloodline has always been one of high esteem throughout the realm. In this time of transition, whilst the Duchess finds her footing, Duke Pettraud wonders if your duchy might consider a son of Pettraud to help you usher in this new era."

Jax fought to keep her face from reflecting the venom coursing through her. She knew exactly what Pettraud wanted, but she needed to hear it said out loud. "Forgive me, Courtier Rence. I think I have found my footing quite well thus far. How would a son of Pettraud be of help?"

At her direct question, Rence looked extremely uncomfortable. Jaquobie, too, narrowed his eyes dangerously, clearly not wanting her to spark a feud. "Well, Your Grace, the Duchy of Pettraud would like to extend an offer of marriage to the Duchess."

Before Jax could respond with a carefully planned retort, silverware clattered to her left.

"Rence?! What is the meaning of this? The lady only just lost her parents, and now you're requesting she marry one of my brothers?" Perry stood abruptly, causing all eyes to focus on him. "Did my father plan this all along?"

Rence, quite shocked by the lack of decorum being displayed, urged Perry to sit down, but the young lord refused until he received an answer. Reluctantly and red-faced, Rence hissed across the table, "Why do you think your father let you go to the Mensina tourney when you've never been allowed out of the duchy before?"

"Me?" Perry gasped, mortified. "He wanted you to offer me, as what? As a coronation gift to the Duchess? Virtues' sake." Running a hand through his dark hair, he pushed himself away from the table in frustration. "Forgive my outburst, Your Grace, but as you can see, the true purpose of this visit was unknown to me until now. I must retire to my rooms for the evening. I bid you goodnight." With a flustered bow, Perry retreated from the hall like a frightened puppy.

Jax struggled to hide her bemusement at how the situation had played out. Of course, she'd felt the same outrage Perry expressed, but she was wise enough to hide it. She couldn't imagine the verbal lashings she'd get from Jaquobie if she even dreamed of behaving in such a way. She sat there in silence, letting her guests fidget.

"Your Grace," Rence finally wheezed, "I cannot begin to apologize for the insubordination you have just witnessed. I am ashamed of our young lord's behavior, and kindly ask that you remember he is still a young lord."

"Just as the Duchess is a young lady." Jaquobie's tone was pointed. She was surprised that he was defending her, reminding Rence that she, too, was young in years, but knew better than to behave like that in front of guests.

"I didn't mean to insinuate that, High Courtier." Rence stumbled across his words. "I have no excuse for his behavior. Ever since the young man lost his mother, he's been very difficult to deal with."

Jax's lips tightened. "So, Duke Pettraud thought that instead of helping his son come to terms with her death, he'd ship him off to be wed to a woman whose own parents had just died?" Her words were harsh. "Is *that* all I am to the Duke? Someone to babysit his son?"

"Virtues, no, Your Grace!" Rence was frantic, near tears, even. "I won't lie and say that it didn't cross his mind that you two may be kindred spirits. That perhaps, you both could help each other deal with your losses. But your father and the Duke have discussed you marrying a Pettraud son for years. It was an agreement they'd established some time ago. The Duke intended to send Lord Pettraud to the Mensina tourney, and then on to Saphire to meet with your father. But then the unthinkable happened…and the Duke adjusted his plans."

Jax sat back in her chair, exhaustion creeping over her. Her first full day as Duchess, and she was ready to toss her hands up in defeat. She couldn't very well back out on an agreement, even an informal one, her father had made with Duke Pettraud. "Courtier Rence, while I don't doubt that the Duke has anything but noble intentions, I am simply not accepting any proposals at this point in time. My reign officially began yesterday, and I'd like some time to adjust to this new life myself."

Jaquobie's eyes flash with disbelief.

Nevertheless, she continued, giving him a silencing look. "I do consider the Duchy of Pettraud to be one of our greatest allies, and I would like to invite Lord Pettraud to stay here as a guest of Saphire for however long the Duke allows. This will give us the opportunity to get to know one another and solidify a marriage proposal at a later date. Does that sound agreeable to you?"

She was certain Rence would have complied with anything she requested in that moment, but her consent to keep marriage on the table nearly had him leaping for joy. "I will inform the Duke of this evening's events to get his approval, but I can say with confidence that this arrangement sounds splendid, Your Grace."

"Wonderful. I will leave it to you to inform Lord Pettraud of his future. My lady-in-waiting will arrange a more permanent apartment for him. We want him to feel at home, after all." Jax stood gracefully from the table, summoning all her remaining energy to depart the room with confidence she did not feel. She had successfully given herself a stay of execution regarding the marriage offer, but she knew that she would have to accept it at some point. Pettraud was indeed one of the strongest allies Saphire had, and she could not risk their trade agreements falling through because of her unwillingness to wed.

High Courtier Jaquobie knew this, and no doubt would have backpedaled the conversation if she had outright refused. As she had been trained, she put her duchy ahead of her own desires, and couldn't help but be pleased by the pride evident in Jaquobie's fierce gaze as she glided out of the room.

She strolled to her quarters alone, hoping Arnie would come find her once she'd secured new rooms in the east wing for Perry. She had so much to tell her, she wasn't sure where to begin. Just mere hours ago, she'd found out her parents had been murdered, the stench of a despicable plot reeking from their corpses. How was she going to get to the bottom of this mess all while playing hostess to her future husband?

The thought of Perry becoming her husband momentarily blindsided her as if she had not fully comprehended until now what she and Rence negotiated. That disaster of a politician would be tied to her, bound to her nation. It would be up to Jax to teach Perry the proper ways to present himself as a royal consort, lessons she was already dreading. She couldn't help but be a little offended that Duke Pettraud had offered his youngest and most inexperienced son as her betrothed. Although, the Duke may actually have been paying her a great compliment. *Here, take my most worthless son as your husband, for you certainly do not need any help ruling in your father's stead.*

Immediately, she winced that she was so quick to judge Perry's value. If anything, in their short conversations together, she thought he was extremely kindhearted and good-natured. Sons of Dukes who had little chance of ascending the throne tended to be arrogant and cunning. Perry didn't have a deceitful bone in his body, or so his outburst revealed. She already considered him a friend; she should be so lucky in her position to marry someone she got along with.

Uma helped her undress and put on her night clothes, neither saying anything substantial. Jax was certain the dining hall staff would have gossiped about the events at dinner, and it was likely Uma knew all about the indecent proposal. Thankfully, her maid knew her place and kept any prying questions to herself.

Sinking into a chair, Jax rubbed her throbbing temples. "See that I'm up before dawn, Uma. I have some work to do before breakfast with our guests."

Uma nodded her understanding and left for the night.

Alone with her thoughts, Jax decided she should seek out Vyanti and see what the autopsies had revealed. A fervent knock on her door interrupted her plans, as Vyanti himself stuck his head into her chambers. Rather than reprimand him for barging in on her—again—she ushered him once more into the sitting room and perched on a chair. "Please tell me you've found something."

He wasted no time in explaining his findings. "It was bloodsleaf, Your Grace. Somehow, your parents drank or ate something laced with bloodsleaf. The poison takes about two or three hours to kill its victim, meaning they could have consumed it either before or after they departed for the Mensina tourney, based on the location the carriage was found."

Jax shivered at the mention of the poison, sounding so dastardly in name. "Could they have possibly stopped somewhere along the way and been poisoned then?"

Master Vyanti shook his head. "Your parents never would have accepted food or drink that was not prepared by the palace. Your guards should have briefed you on this when explaining how your travel security works now that you are Duchess."

She frowned, searching for the memory. The Captain of the Ducal Guard's stern face came into view, and she recalled him detailing the lengthy royal carriage protocols. "So, we can conclusively determine that the poison must have come from the palace?"

Master Vyanti nodded. "Yes, I am afraid so. However, we

cannot know for certain *when* they digested the toxin. Perhaps the moment they entered the carriage and left the palace grounds, it took hold of them, meaning that they could have been poisoned three hours before they even left the castle."

Jax scrunched her nose in disappointment. It was quite a large window of time to investigate. "I'll ask for a detailed account of my parents' movements that morning. I don't believe anyone was ever questioned back at the palace because it was deemed an accidental crash."

Vyanti leaned forward. "Agreed, Your Grace, but you must be careful. You cannot raise suspicions as to why you're asking these questions."

Jax pondered a moment. "I could have Arnie ask in my place."

The physician's reaction surprised her. "No, Your Grace. I know you trust Arnie with your life, but this secret must be kept between the two of us. I know Arnie would never willingly betray your confidence, but it is no secret that she admires the Earl of Crepsta, who had brothers visiting Saphire at the time…" he trailed off, not wanting to voice his concerns any further.

"You think this is a plot by one of the other duchies?" Jax gave a sharp intake of breath.

"We do not know anything for certain. But we could put Arnie in harm's way if Crepsta was behind this, especially if they caught wind you knew the truth and confided in her." Master Vyanti's words were urgent.

Jax sat back, processing it all. Vyanti's pleas made perfect sense, and she'd never want to put Arnie in danger. But the thought that Crepsta could be behind this, and more so, the thought of keeping this monumental secret to herself, made Jax feel hopelessly alone. "You have my word I will keep this between the two of us."

Satisfied with her declaration, the elderly man pushed himself out of the chair and headed for the door. "I'll see if I can figure out how our assassin came to acquire bloodsleaf. It is not a common specimen, nor is it grown in our region. It would have been purchased from an herbalist or merchant in the market."

"Meet me tomorrow night with your findings, Master Vyanti. Come after Uma has readied me for bed," Jax instructed, blowing out the few candles lighting her room.

With a click of the door, the physician departed, and she was at long last, alone.

Falling into the embrace of her pillows, Jax sighed, worried that sleep would elude her tonight. But with dark images of bloodsleaf buzzing through her head, she fell into a tortured, but deep slumber.

Chapter Five

"Your Grace, you requested I wake you early today."

Uma's prim voice strummed softly at her consciousness, slowly pulling Jax out of the black storm clouds shadowing her nightmares. While she still felt incredibly tired, morning had not come soon enough for her liking.

"Thank you, Uma." She yawned as she swung her feet onto the cool floor. Her fireplace had gone out in the night, leaving her room to fall victim the chilly spring weather. Uma was already placing logs in the hearth. "No need to stoke the fire just yet, Uma. I shan't be in my chambers much today."

Uma scuttled away from the stone structure, bringing Jax a light green gown for the day. It was elegant enough to wear to breakfast with the Pettraud delegation but also comfortable for whatever work her day had in store. Uma knew her tastes and desires so well, it almost spooked her.

Quickly securing the lace backing and braiding Jax's long, honeyed hair, Uma placed the Duchess's informal crown in her soft tresses. Informal in that the crown only boasted one prominent sapphire gem.

Looking much more refreshed than she felt, Jax smiled at her maid and bid her farewell for the morning. Heading to the courtyard, she guessed she would be able to watch dawn break over Sephretta. While the sunrise was not her reason for walking the gardens, it gave her a good excuse if anyone asked why she was up and about so early.

Just as she expected, the Captain of the Ducal Guard had stationed himself under one of the trellis archways, his eyes focused on the courtyard's main entrance. George Solomon, a seasoned warrior at age thirty-five, had been her father's most trusted guardsman, having served the duchy since he was sixteen. Jax remembered her youthful daydreams about running away with the dark, steadfast soldier, blushing at her ridiculous plans. Her mother would have died of embarrassment if her daughter married a commoner, regardless of his high-ranking station.

At least her childhood fantasies had not been completely crushed. Captain Solomon became one of her closest friends and confidantes as she matured into her twenties, often escorting her from duchy to duchy during her travels.

His deep brown eyes were so focused on his post that he jumped when she approached him. "Goodness, Jax, what are you doing up this early?"

She smiled coyly. "I wanted to talk with you, and I know that you prefer to stand duty at dawn."

He chuckled, completely disregarding all protocol of how a guardsman should act around a Duchess. "I hope you have come to tell me firsthand how last night actually played out. The stories around the palace are wild."

Huffing in mock indignation, she chided him. "I cannot believe the staff is gossiping." She fluttered around him, all light and airy. "Especially when the truth is stranger than fiction." She shared with him an elegantly woven tale about Rence's proposal and Perry's outburst, and how it had all resulted in Perry being a permanent guest of Saphire.

"Your first day as Duchess, and you've already secured yourself a match. Quite the feat, Your Grace."

If it had been anyone but Captain Solomon, she would have reprimanded them for their candor, but she simply laughed with her friend. As her story sank in between the two of them, she sobered. "It's absurd, that's what it is...Lord Pettraud is certainly not who I expected to be bound to." She risked a glance at the

Captain, curious to see his reaction to her cryptic words.

Something unreadable flickered in his chocolate eyes as he cleared his throat. "Having expectations about one's life always ends in disappointment, I find."

She wished her blossoming cheeks weren't so incriminating. She wondered if the Captain was referring to the same incident that pushed its way to the forefront of her mind now. How foolish she'd once been, thinking she could convince her father's most loyal soldier to run away with her. She'd just turned nineteen and desperately wanted to leave Saphire behind. Under the romantic cover of darkness, she'd confessed her feelings to a twenty-six-year-old George Solomon. Ever the gentleman, he had let her down easy, reminding her of the oath he took to protect the Crown, that he couldn't abandon his post, no matter much he wanted to. She'd taken comfort in knowing he admired her even if he couldn't break his vow. She'd cherished his words in the weeks after her impulsive confession, using them to bandage raw wounds. Eventually, her lusty desires had succumbed to time and a strong friendship had grown in its place.

Brushing the surprisingly vivid memory aside, Jax gave the Captain a cavalier smirk. "Duke Pettraud certainly won't get the power he expects out of the deal."

Her friend rearranged his features and tenderly reached out. "Your father would be proud of how you handled it all, Jax. You know that, right?"

Startled by his change in tone, she nodded her head solemnly. "He always told me how much he wished I could marry for love. Perhaps Perry will surprise us all." She looked off into the distance, watching the morning shadows creep over the sleeping land. "I actually have something else I'd like to ask you, George." She used the Captain's first name, signaling that this was a discussion to be kept in confidence.

"Anything. What is it?" He pushed his dark, thick hair from his eyes, giving her his full attention.

"It's just…" she trailed off for a moment, unsure of how to best proceed, "I was hoping you could tell me a bit about the morning before my parents left for Mensina. Were they happy? Did they laugh at breakfast at all? I want to remember them, knowing they enjoyed their final hours before everything went wrong."

Captain Solomon's broad shoulders sagged. Jax knew he blamed himself for the carriage accident, guilt-ridden that his men had failed to protect the Duke and Duchess. "Of course, Your Grace. They were obviously excited to have a short respite from affairs of state. Your mother was looking forward to seeing her sisters. Your father opted out of joining her for breakfast because he and I had some reports to look over and approve before his departure. We were in his study for most of the morning before Jaquobie came to collect your father. Your parents took off in their carriage not ten minutes later."

Jax tried to keep a frown off her face. "My father didn't take breakfast? That's his favorite meal of the day," she lied, trying to uncover when her father could have ingested poison that morning.

If he sensed anything odd in her line of questioning, Captain Solomon didn't point it out. "He said he would eat in the carriage. Traveling always made him hungry. He didn't touch any provisions the staff brought to his study."

"How long did you get to spend with him? In his study, I mean?" Jax's tone was wistful, something she didn't have to fake. She would give anything to spend time with her father in his study again.

The Captain shrugged. "I'd say we were in there for at least two hours or more." He lowered his voice. "It pains me that I got to spend so much time with him that day, while you didn't." His brown eyes were damp.

Jax hardly heard his consoling words but took her cue from his demeanor. "He valued you greatly, George. Never forget that." She placed a reassuring hand on his shoulder. "Thank you for sharing my father's remaining hours with me. Do you happen to know if my mother took breakfast with anyone? I'd love to know how she spent her time." She hoped she didn't sound too eager.

"I'm afraid I don't, Jax. Uma might be able to tell you who was serving in the banquet hall that morning," he pointed out.

"Excellent idea, George. Thank you ever so much." She gave him a quick kiss on the cheek before rushing out of the gardens to find her next target.

Based on what she had learned, her mother and father were separated for at least two hours that morning before they entered the carriage. It was possible that the bloodsleaf had been slipped into their bedside water goblets and they'd drank it when they woke, but the poison's timeframe didn't work in favor of that theory. Master Vyanti said it would take two to three hours for the toxin to claim its victims. If she could figure out what her mother's movements were, she could determine whether or not the poison had been ingested after they entered the carriage.

It appeared, based on George's memory, that her father had not had anything to eat or drink in the hours before his departure. She wondered if it was possible for Vyanti to tell if her parents died around the same time. Perhaps her mother drank the poison long before her father did, causing her to pass away first. She also wanted to know what kind of side effects bloodsleaf caused. Captain Solomon didn't mention her father acting oddly at all. Either the poison surprises its victim with death, or the side effects did not begin to show until an hour or two after consuming it. She cursed under her breath that she'd have to wait until tonight to confer with the physician. He'd no doubt already be on his way out of the castle to see if he could find the bloodsleaf's origin.

†

Uma looked surprised, and perhaps a little embarrassed, when Jax knocked on her door and barged into the maid's sitting room. "Your Grace? Is there something you need?" She stood up and curtsied next to her desk chair.

Jax sat down on a worn cushion, taking in the small, but tastefully decorated quarters. "Yes, Uma, sorry to pop in like this, but I have something to ask. I was wondering if you could tell me who attended my mother in the banquet hall the morning of the accident. I just want to make sure her final hours were happy." She brushed her skirts, fidgeting under Uma's questioning gaze.

Uma straightened the papers she'd been writing on, tucking them away in her desk. "Soren attends to the banquet hall when there is not a formal meal taking place. She would have overseen and served your mother, I believe."

"Soren? Where might I find her?" Jax stood up to leave, impatient to get to the next piece of the puzzle.

"I think you'll find her in the pantry at this hour. She helps the baker when she's not on the floor." Uma explained to Jax where the pantry was located, for it had been a long time since Jax had been anywhere near the kitchens to sneak a treat. With a thankful smile, Jax left her lady's maid to whatever she had been working on.

‡

"I'm looking for Soren. Has anyone seen her?" Jax bellowed as she entered the lively kitchen, the smell of banana bread pudding wafting through the air. Her stomach grumbled, reminding her she had not yet stopped for breakfast.

"Your Grace!" Her appearance sent the bustling kitchen workers into a frenzy, bowing and tripping over themselves. She waved a hand in greeting, reassuring them all that they should not mind the disruption.

The executive chef waddled over, covered in flour and cocoa

powder. "To what do we owe the honor, Duchess?" he asked after a flourishing bow.

"Soren. I need a word with her," Jax reiterated her request, trying to keep her tone friendly and light.

"She'll be right through that side door, Your Grace." The chef pointed at a heavy door in the back of the room. "She's helping prepare the pastries for the Pettraud delegation's breakfast."

"Thank you, sir." Jax didn't bother reading the name embroidered on the chef's jacket. She squeezed her way through the commotion of flaming stoves, hot trays, and chopped ingredients. The clamor died down behind her as she entered the small room and shut the heavy door. The pantry was much quieter. Only the sound of dough being kneaded danced on the cool air. "Soren? May I have a word?"

Of the six or so people in the room who looked up at her with a startled expression, only one approached. Soren was a rail-thin, middle-aged woman who must have been almost six feet tall. Her salt and pepper brown hair was tucked under a bonnet, her pale face flushing with color. "Your Grace? How may I be of service?"

Jax looked around, mindful of the ears and eyes narrowed in on them. "Is there someplace private you and I may chat?"

Soren nervously nodded, leading Jax through yet another heavy door and into a deserted sitting area. "We won't be bothered in here, Your Grace."

Jax took in the scene, having no doubt that the entire kitchen staff was waiting eagerly on the other side of the door, thirsting for gossip. "I was hoping you may recall serving my mother breakfast the morning of her accident."

Soren looked confused at the direction of her inquiry. "Why, yes, ma'am, I remember my last morning with the Duchess as if it were yesterday."

Jax leaned towards the woman, putting a hand gently on her trembling arm. "Soren, I am desperate to hear of my mother's final hours before her untimely death. It would give me such peace to know that she was happy and enjoyed herself before..." she trailed off suggestively.

"Of course, ma'am, completely understandable. Your mother was very excited to visit her sisters. She mainly talked about how long it had been since the Mensina daughters had all been together in one room. She mentioned she would be meeting several nephews and nieces for the first time."

Jax nodded with interest, coaxing the woman on. "I know Mother loved those apple donuts the bakers make. Is that what she had to eat for her final meal?"

Soren's brow furrowed a bit, and Jax knew her question sounded forced. "I believe your mother had toast and eggs, nothing fancy, just like she requested. She had some fruit juice and coffee, and that was about it."

Jax paused for a moment before pressing for more details. "Anything else you can tell me, anything that might have seemed...I don't know...unusual?"

"Unusual? I don't know what you mean." Soren's back stiffened.

Jax backpedaled, not wanting the woman to think she was accusing her of anything. "Mother sometimes got herself worked up too much when she was excited. She didn't appear ill in any way, did she? It ruined her spirits when she got like that."

Soren let out a sigh of relief. "Oh, no, your mother was in perfect health throughout the whole meal. She stayed in the banquet hall reading her morning briefing until she was collected by the Duke."

Jax strode gracefully around the room, puzzling over what Soren had shared. "I'm glad she was untroubled. It's nicer for me to remember her that way, rather than after the accident."

Soren bowed once more. "Of course, Your Grace. I am pleased I could be of some assistance."

Jax dismissed the woman, plopping down on one of the hard-wooden chairs when she was alone. So, her mother had an uneventful morning, too. She needed to get in touch with Vyanti to figure out if her mother would have displayed signs of poisoning. If so, then Soren's account would align with the theory that her parents had been poisoned *after* entering the carriage.

Leaving the kitchens through a side door, Jax avoided the rampant gossip that was no doubt taking place amongst the servants. She wound her way through a myriad of corridors, directing herself toward the banquet hall where she would soon be hosting breakfast. She replayed her findings in her head, so consumed with determining when the poisoning occurred that she collided with a distracted Lord Pettraud.

"Goodness, Your Grace, my sincerest apologies!" Perry exclaimed, helping Jax steady herself with his strong grip.

She stepped back and brushed the wrinkles out of her skirts. "No need to apologize, Perry. I was the one at fault. I was so lost in thought, I didn't even see you there." She hated appearing frazzled in front of a guest. "I'm on my way to breakfast. Would you like to join me?"

Perry bowed, extending his arm. "Of course, but I'd like to have a word with you privately beforehand if you wouldn't mind?" His kind, lavender eyes were lined with worry.

"Were your rooms not acceptable?" Jax asked, unsure where the conversation was heading.

"My new apartment is fine. T-thank you so much for the hospitality." Perry stuttered his words nervously. "I actually wanted to speak to you about last night's events. I am ashamed by my reaction, but I am actually more abhorred that my father would be so callous as to extend a marriage proposal while you are in mourning. I hope you can forgive Pettraud for the imprudence."

"There is nothing to forgive. I am sure the Duke had the best intentions," Jax responded, although she doubted the sincerity in her words.

Perry chuckled darkly. "Oh, the Duke and his intentions. I'm still stunned that he would send his youngest son off as an offering, like a chest of gold. I knew he was not pleased with my behavior of late, but I never thought he'd punish me in such a way."

Jax answered his statement coolly. "I'd like to think that my hand in marriage would not be a punishment, but rather an honor, Lord Pettraud."

His handsome face drained of color, and he comically slapped himself on the forehead. "Virtues, that's not what I meant to imply at all." He looked at her with such sadness in his eyes that she was momentarily speechless. "I'm sure you have heard about the death of my mother."

She nodded sympathetically. "Yes, I am very sorry for your loss, Perry. My parents attended her funeral to show their condolences. I, unfortunately, was visiting the southern shore of Savant, and could not attend the service in time."

If he heard her excuse, he did not acknowledge it. "My mother was the one person who believed I was worth something. Being the seventh son, the last in the line of succession, my father hardly had any time for me, always training and working with my older brothers. But my mother, Virtues bless her, she loved me despite my standing. She was the only person in my family that encouraged me to be a better man than I was the day before. And with her gone, it all seems hopeless."

Jax appraised the young man before her and for the first time, saw past his charisma and charm to see a lonely little boy who yearned for his father's approval, knowing deep down, he would never achieve it. It was a vicious side effect of royal life. "I'm sure your mother is looking down on you, Perry, and she wants you to be happy. You cannot give up just because she isn't physically here anymore. I'm sure you'll find your worth, and as long as you are here in Saphire, I will help you."

54

Perry reached for her hand and squeezed it gently. "That's very kind of you, Duchess. I hope I am able to prove myself to you."

They stood in silence for an awkward moment, before Jax cleared her throat. "What are you passionate about? That is always the best place to start."

Perry examined her eyes thoughtfully as he pondered her question. "Well, my mother knew how much I loved riding horses as a young boy, so she convinced my father to allow me to joust. It's not the fighting I enjoy, as much as riding those majestic beasts."

"Our stables are world-class, Perry. You must take advantage of them," Jax suggested, delighted to see a spark of interest in his gaze.

"I'm also very fond of painting, as silly as it might sound." Perry glanced at the ground, blushing.

"Not at all. You and Arnie must chat with one another. She enjoys the art, too. In fact, she's painted a few of the royal portraits hanging in these great halls." Jax motioned to the high walls around them, showing off the extensive collection the Duchy of Saphire had accrued.

"Excellent, yes, I must speak with her. Although, I prefer to capture the beauty of nature. You know, when dawn stretches across an undisturbed field, or stars sing across the tops of mountains. Saphire's lands are magnificent, so I'm sure I'll find something worthy of my canvas." Perry's eyes glazed over as he detailed for her the scenes he longed to capture.

"I cannot wait to see what you create." She squeezed his arm affectionately, looking him over. Considering his extremely good looks and affable manner, she felt a touch of hope that this marriage might make her happy in the end.

Upon their arrival at the banquet hall, the rest of the Pettraud group fell silent, Rence's raised eyebrows prominent in the crowd. She could see the glee in his expression, for he'd likely report back to Duke Pettraud that his son was already wooing the Duchess.

While she skillfully planned for the courtier to witness her fawning at the young lord's side, she found that her admiration was not entirely forced. Perry's candidness about the devastating loss of his mother pulled at her heartstrings, and she was moved by his resolution to make her proud. Rence would, no doubt, report to Duke Pettraud that their courtship was moving quickly in the right direction.

"Good morning, I hope you all slept well." Jax let her voice float musically around all her guests. She directed Perry to sit on her right, whilst Arnie emerged from the back of the hall and took a seat at her left.

"I thought you'd never get here and I'd be stuck with these buffoons all morning," her lady-in-waiting murmured, her eyes annoyingly directed at the congregation of tourney knights.

Before Jax could sneak a snarky reply, Rence sat down beside Perry. "A most good morning to you, Your Illustrious Highness."

Jax fought back a snort at the use of her title in such an informal setting. "Greetings, Courtier Rence. I hope you feel rested for your journey." While her tone was friendly and light, she could see that Rence understood her true intentions. She was ready for the delegation to return home and leave her be.

"Yes, a good night's sleep on a dovetail mattress has done wonders for these aging bones." Rence lowered his head in understanding. "Lord Pettraud, I trust your permanent quarters were to your satisfaction?" He inquired after the welfare of his charge.

"I was just telling the Illustrious Duchess here that I have never seen such splendor." Perry sent a conspiratorial look her way, grinning mischievously.

Beside her, Arnie struggled not to spit out her juice as she laughed. Jax placed her napkin on her lap, not making further eye contact with the incorrigible crew.

Perry turned toward his courtier. "I expect that we'll be

receiving news from Father once you've explained the arrangement the Duchess has agreed to?" His mood darkened a trace, a change not lost on Jax.

Rence cleared his throat, clearly aware he was at odds with this end of the table. "I'm sure your father will want someone to check in on you to make sure all is going well."

Perry frowned. "You mean, to check to see if the Duchess has thrown me into the dungeons for my lack of decorum?"

Rence sputtered at the assumption, but Perry did not allow him to continue. "I trust it won't be a burden, Duchess, to host another party from our duchy? Duke Pettraud will likely be very particular about how things play out between us, you see."

Jax understood immediately what Perry was alluding to. Duke Pettraud, despite her verbal agreement, would want to send representatives to monitor this period of courtship to ensure his son did nothing to upset his chances of marriage. Where she couldn't very well refuse to accommodate visitors, she was basically going to be under a microscope the entire time. She shouldn't have expected anything less. "We will be honored to welcome any delegation of Pettraud, whenever they see fit." She directed her words to Rence, hoping the courtier would share her willingness to comply with the Duke. "But let it also be known that I have great faith in the arrangement." She shared a small smile with Perry, whose ears grew pink.

The rest of breakfast was rather quiet, the whole room too afraid to poke a hole in the budding relationship between the young lord and Duchess. Jax was thankful when Rence announced he and the knights should be on their way, and she bid him goodbye from the banquet hall, putting Arnie in charge of escorting the group out of the palace.

‡

"I hope you don't mind some constructive criticism, Perry," Jax broached the delicate subject, "but when you sit as a guest of my table, I suggest you try to keep your temper in check."

Strolling the gardens, taking in the brilliant spring sunlight, the young man turned to look at her head on. "Are you about to lecture me on my behavior?" Surprisingly, his tone was that of amusement and not annoyance.

Jax blushed, wringing her hands. "Perhaps?"

"All right, then. Let me have it." Perry crossed his arms, expectantly.

"Well, it's just, if you ever speak to any of my personal guests the way you spoke to Rence or behave the way you did last night, I *will* have you thrown in the dungeon." She delivered her cutting words dryly, hoping to be crystal clear.

Perry's face reddened as he processed her statement, but to her surprise, he released a long sigh. "Rest assured, I will be on my very best behavior going forward, Your Grace." He used her title in a defeated manner.

Jax reached out to touch him. "You must realize that there are times when I must speak as a Duchess and not your friend. Going forward, the stakes will be much higher than they were at last night's dinner. I will be hosting rulers from across the entire realm, and I cannot have flippant remarks made by the man I intend to marry."

Perry looked at her strangely. "You really do intend to see this through? It's not just an act to keep my father at bay?"

Jax's eyes darkened. "I gave Courtier Rence my word that, after a time, I would be ready to accept this marriage arrangement. I am a woman of my word, Lord Pettraud."

At the use of his title, Perry cringed. "I almost feel bad for you that you're stuck with me."

"Almost?" Jax raised an eyebrow.

Perry grinned, poking her playfully in the side. "Well, I am stuck with you, after all."

Chapter Six

Jax and Perry spent much of the day together, touring the castle grounds while sharing stories from their childhoods, getting to know one another better. She wanted him to feel free to roam as he pleased and felt a guided tour would help him grow accustomed to the layout. Jax joked that she often got lost in the winding halls, as she'd spent so much of her life away from the palace.

"Why?" Perry asked, genuinely interested. "Why did you stay away from home so much?"

Jax gnawed on her lip, unsure if she'd ever voiced her reasons out loud. "When I was younger, I didn't want anything to do with the life that came along with being the Duke of Saphire's heir. I know some people dream of being a princess, but they only know the half of it...the part we show to our people. The glamour and finery, it's all an act." She sighed, glancing down at her feet in shame for taking her wealth and power for granted. "All the balls and public appearances...it got old rather quick. I convinced my father I wanted to be a scholar, that going to the Academy would help me mature into a more just and fair ruler."

"You must have done quite some persuading. It's unusual for a *female* heir to a duchy to attend the Academy." Perry's brow furrowed as he likely reflected on the odd custom.

An unrefined snort escaped her. "My father, luckily, shared the same views as I did when it came to gender double standards. He eventually agreed to my proposition, and off I went." Her eyes clouded over with memories of her days roaming the historic institution, scurrying with Arnie from class to class. "I excelled in political science and economics, so upon my graduation, my father appointed me as his ambassador, hoping to strengthen our nation's relationships across the realm. And it did. I'm very proud of the work I have accomplished for my duchy, even before I became Duchess."

Perry watched her intently. "Do you regret it?"

The soft concern behind his words made her regal façade begin to crumble. "I don't know, honestly. If I had known what little time I would have with my parents…I might have gone a different route. But I was a difficult child, too, forever lashing out at my mother. She was the enforcer, you see. She'd grown up in a far stricter household than my father, and she had high expectations for her daughter. She practically had to drag me to every party or event, showing me off like a trophy." A quiver of remorse ran down her spine. She could have made things easier for her mother by just obeying. "Sending me to the Academy mended our relationship in many ways because we were no longer at each other's throats day in and day out. I learned so much there and gained the confidence I needed to be a good sovereign. Without my training, I'm not sure I would have been suitable for the position." Her brutal honesty fueling her admission shocked her, but Perry did not flinch.

"You will be a great ruler." He reached out and took her hand in his, calming warmth trickling up her fingers. "Of that, I am certain."

Blushing, Jax turned away and noticed Arnie approaching from one of the garden paths.

As she reached them, Arnie curtsied, her skirts sweeping across the dewy grass.

Perry tipped his chin in return greeting. "Lady Aranelda! Are you enjoying this glorious spring day as much as I am?"

"Please, call me Arnie. Aranelda makes me sound like a wicked old witch." Her friend chuckled, tossing her hair over her shoulder. "I've come to find you, Lord Pettraud. The Duchess tells me you are an artist. I hope my paint collection will suffice until more can be brought up from the market."

Perry's eyes brightened. "I'm sure your assortment will put mine back home to shame. My father was never one to approve of this little hobby, and thus, I had to make do with creating my own dyes in secret." He winked at his companions.

"Arnie, why don't you get our guest set up while I work through some rather boring state business," Jax suggested lightly, giving both their cue to leave. She'd dallied with her future consort long enough for today. She had a duchy to attend to. "I shall see you at supper."

Perry looked moderately discouraged to be dismissed but took it in stride. "Until then, my lady." With a tender kiss on the cheek, he backed away, his eyes yearning for more.

She watched her friends stroll away, pleased to find their temperaments were so compatible. She had yet to spend quality time with Arnie to discuss all the goings on, but at least her two friends seemed to be getting along well.

Ten minutes later, she arrived at the study that had once belonged to her father and sat down wearily behind the grand mahogany desk. Alone with her thoughts, her focus shifted back to the two bodies floors below her. Fear seeped into her veins. She couldn't risk anyone finding out her parents had been murdered, or Saphire would be seen as weak and vulnerable. What's more, how would she conduct a proper investigation into her parents' murders if she was being watched by Duke Pettraud's spies the entire time? She needed to get to the bottom of things before the Duke sent anyone to check up on her courtship with Perry.

Shuffling a pile of paperwork, Jax absentmindedly went about her more tedious duties, only to be interrupted a few hours later by a knock on her door. Frowning, her eyes flashed to the intruder but her demeanor changed when she found an elderly figure standing in the shadows.

"Master Vyanti! What news do you have?" She had not been

expecting the physician to reappear until later that night.

He scurried to her side, his eyes wild. "I know I said I would come to you in the evening, Your Grace, but I decided to share what I've come across before I head back down to the marketplace. I have learned much this day."

"As have I." Jax twisted herself in her chair, clasping her hands eagerly. "I spoke with Captain Solomon and one of the kitchen maids, as they spent the morning of the accident with my parents. George said my father ate no food in his presence, and they were together two hours prior to his immediate departure. Soren, the maid, said my mother had eggs, toast, and juice from the kitchen and was in the best of spirits."

The old man's eyes piqued with interest. "I think I know where you are going with this line of questioning. Your mother displayed no obvious symptoms that she had been poisoned during her morning routine."

"Exactly!" Jax exclaimed.

"And you are correct, there would have been symptoms once the poison entered the bloodstream. Your parents would have started to complain of headaches and immense fatigue within the hour. Then vomiting would occur, followed by a coma leading to death." The old man massaged his temples, as if warding off a headache of his own. "After my analysis of their bodies, I can conclusively say they died around the same time."

Jax closed her eyes, not wanting to think about her parents falling victim to the savage bloodsleaf. It made her blood boil that they were forced to endure such pain before their lives were taken. They must have been so afraid and confused, helpless as they watched the poison take hold of one another. "Based on what we've learned, they must have been poisoned after they boarded the carriage. If only their guards had survived…we could have asked them when the Duke and Duchess started acting ill."

Master Vyanti folded his arms. "Well, on that front, I do have some helpful news. I autopsied the bodies of the quad that was assigned to escort them, and all four men were also poisoned."

"How is that helpful?" Jax's stomach flipped at the notion.

"On my way to the Sephretta marketplace this morning, I took a detour and instead, stopped by a tavern that was on their route to Mensina. Your parents did not get off their carriage, but the innkeeper remembered two of the guards coming in to use their washroom." Master Vyanti's lips curled triumphantly. "The innkeeper said they looked absolutely dreadful—like they had the plague. He made them use the basins outside."

"Where is this tavern located?"

"From the palace, it took me about an hour on horseback. The carriage would have moved at a much slower pace. Your parents would have likely reached it two hours after departing the castle." The physician explained his calculations to her.

Jax tapped her chin as she puzzled through the timeline. "So, by that time, at least two of the guards were showing symptoms of the poison."

Vyanti nodded. "And based on the symptoms the innkeeper described, they would have died within the hour of leaving the tavern. Considering all four bodies of the guards were found under or around the crashed carriage, it's likely that once the poison had taken its toll, the group was ambushed. The perpetrators then relocated the bodies, staging the carriage crash."

"Why do you think they were relocated?"

"Because the wreckage was found more than an hour's ride away from the inn. It would have been impossible for the sick group to make it that far."

Jax opened one of her desk drawers and pulled out a map. "Could you mark for me where the tavern is and where the carriage was found, please?"

Dutifully, the physician took a quill pen and scratched two X's on the map. Jax studied at their locations relative to one another. "I have an idea." She measured the site. "You head to the marketplace as planned and let me know what you find out about the bloodsleaf. I'll ride out to the tavern and continue on the route my parents' carriage would have taken to Mensina. They could have been ambushed anywhere along that path. Captain Solomon and his men only searched the immediate wreckage area. It's possible our assassins may have left some clues behind at the ambush site."

Master Vyanti's brow furrowed. "I know we said to keep this between us, Your Grace, but it's highly imprudent for you to go out there on your own."

Jax raked her brain for an excuse, one finally springing to mind. "I won't go alone, then."

✝

Dinner that night was much more enjoyable than the delegation feast the previous night. Perry was her only dining companion. Earlier in the afternoon, Arnie stated with a coy gleam that she preferred to dine in her room alone. The obnoxious wink she gave Jax made her chuckle at her friend's matchmaking instincts.

"So, day one. How did you fair? Was it pure torture?" Jax joked as Perry stuffed his mouth with duck breast.

"Horrible." He grinned through his food. "I won't say it was complete torture. I got to spend my morning strolling around with a gorgeous woman and my afternoon painting with another beautiful lady."

Jax smiled, shaking her finger at him. "Don't go getting your heart set on another woman, Pettraud. Especially one who is taken."

Perry looked surprised. "Arnie is engaged?"

Jax waved her hand flippantly. "Not officially, but I'm expecting Duke Crepsta to make the offer on behalf of his nephew soon."

Her companion chewed thoughtfully. "Hmm, she didn't mention that..."

For some reason, a stab of jealousy ripped through Jax's chest at Perry's concern.

He must have sensed it, for he held his arms up in protest. "No, goodness, that's not what I meant—I thought she might get along with my brother Kaul. He's sixth in line for the Pettraud throne, so if they married and he was bequeathed some Saphire lands, he could make his home here, so Arnie wouldn't have to leave you."

Touched by the consideration he displayed, Jax reached across her place setting and took his hand. "I appreciate you brokering my friend's marriage options, but I will not let my own desires get in the way of her marrying for true love. She and the Earl fell for each other the moment they met at the Academy, even though their courtship has been a little rocky. I could never ask her to give that up for me." She didn't mean to sound so upset, but she had a hard time containing her mounting dread over the imminent departure of her best friend.

"I didn't realize it was true love, Your Grace. Of course, nothing should stand in its way," Perry commented, smiling softly. He squeezed her hand and kissed it affectionately before letting her return to her supper.

In the silence that followed, Jax realized she would never have the luxury of finding her true love. Her partner sat before her, and while she was growing rather fond of him by the minute, true love was just a dream.

"Perry, I have an idea," she declared, shaking her head free of romantic delusions. "Why don't you and I go for a ride tomorrow? I can show you some of the most beautiful sights in Saphire." She popped a juicy grape into her mouth.

"I couldn't think of anything I'd enjoy more," Perry proclaimed, sipping his wine with enthusiasm.

Jax bit into a piece of chocolate cake with triumph. "Wonderful, we shall depart after breakfast."

Chapter Seven

Vyanti barely knocked on the door before she opened it, ushering the man into her chambers. Clad in her nightgown, Jax motioned to the chairs next to the simmering fireplace, fearing that lighting any candles would alert the staff she was awake and moving about. "Any luck finding the source of the bloodsleaf?" she asked through a yawn. It was nearly midnight.

Vyanti, looking incredibly tired from his day of investigation, shook his head discouragingly. "Not a single herbalist or merchant in the marketplace claims to have ever sold it. The only lead I have is that there is a Cetachi tradesman who comes to Sephretta once a week who may sell it. The merchants suspect he'll be arriving either tomorrow or the day after."

"Cetachi? Does bloodsleaf come from that region?" Jax resisted the chill running through her veins. Cetachi was a land of wild men and rebels, refusing to bend to the rule of law. It was the only area of the continent not under ducal leadership.

"I don't have an official register regarding Cetachi's natural resources, but the swampy, cold environment would most certainly allow for the plant to flourish." Vyanti clutched his hands together in contemplation. "I will go back to the market tomorrow and wait for this man."

Jax stood up and hastened to her bureau, lifting the top off a gold jewelry box. "Take this with you and get yourself a room for the evening. I can see that all this traveling is taking its toll on you. You're not as young as you were when you chased me around the west wing, trying to give me those awful serums." She dropped ten nuggets of gold into his outstretched hand, confident that the currency would buy him a comfortable room.

Vyanti scoffed. "Those serums helped you ward off the flu each winter." On a more somber note, he said, "I'm touched by your concern, Jacqueline." His wrinkles multiplied as he gave her a fatherly smile. "I know you think there is a chasm between us because of my faith, but despite it all, you have been very good to me."

She sank into her chair by the fire, the light flickering across her exposed skin. "You will be all right, won't you? You're my only ally in this matter, and I cannot afford to lose you." She assessed the man's sallow face with care.

The old man waved her worries aside, stubborn in his old age. "I'm just a bit winded from all the back and forth travel. I shall take it easy tomorrow."

"But what about this Cetachi merchant? He won't be dangerous, will he?"

Vyanti sputtered in retort. "The Cetachi are harmless. All they want to do is live on their own land, free to have their own beliefs, in peace."

Jax couldn't help but wonder if Vyanti was speaking more about the struggles the Ancient Faith faced in the world. In many duchies, the religion had been scorned into extinction. Saphire was one of the only duchies proclaiming tolerance for those who believed in the old gods. Perhaps Cetachi, a land without laws, structure, or political interference, seemed like a refuge to the court physician. "Still, why don't you take an escort with you? Just in case."

Vyanti's shoulders sagged with resignation. "Very well. I'll agree to an escort, in case someone suspects I've figured out the Duke and Duchess were poisoned."

Jax jumped in her chair at the thought. "But we've been so careful."

"Your questions, while discreet and well-veiled, have been

flying around the gossip chains within the castle." Vyanti did not meet her wide-eyed gaze. "Yes…everyone thinks you're the grieving daughter, but if our culprit knows you are asking questions, they might be able to put two and two together, Your Grace."

Jax growled, flinging herself back against the chair's embrace. "You'd think they'd be chattering about our new guest from Pettraud or something."

The master smiled sadly, sympathizing with her scrutinized life. "You came down to the kitchens, Your Grace. I don't think your father did that in all the years he was Duke. It will probably fuel the staff's conversations for the next week or so."

Jax sat up, flicking her braided hair over her shoulder. "I'll just have to do something that forces them to talk about something else." She quickly revealed her plan to go horseback riding with Lord Pettraud as an excuse to inspect the tavern where her parents' escorts were last seen. "If time allows, I'll see if I can track down the site of the ambush."

Vyanti stood up slowly, taking his leave. "Be careful, my dear. Take Captain Solomon with you. I know this young lord appears innocent and good, but if your parents were killed by another nation, who is to say the extent of the duchies involved."

Jax did not respond as the elderly man shuffled out of the room. The notion that Pettraud—one of her closest allies—could possibly be behind this crime shocked her into silence. As much as it frightened her, any duchy could be a part of the plot. Curling up into her welcoming bed, Jax trembled at the lonely hurt prodding her heart.

Chapter Eight

Clad in her most attractive riding gown, Jax summoned her inner strength as she entered the banquet hall the next morning.

Perry leaped from his chair into a refined bow, his eyes appraising her intricately stitched emerald-and-gold riding ensemble. "You look simply stunning, Jax. I didn't realize this was such a formal event."

She chuckled at the naiveté behind the compliment. "Maybe not for you, Perry, but this will be the first time I've been outside the palace walls since my coronation. I have to make sure my people are impressed by their new Duchess." She patted her hair, which Uma had pinned back in a bun, away from her face.

"They'd have to be blind not to bask in your radiance," he murmured, a longing in his expression.

Jax watched him for a moment, pleased she had such an effect on him this early in their courtship. There was no denying their chemistry.

"Captain Solomon will be accompanying us for protection, but he has assured me he will keep his distance so you and I can continue our conversations from yesterday." Jax waited while her servants prepared a plate of candied toast and ham.

Perry's face fell, but he quickly recovered. "I suppose not having seen my skills as a knight, you would be hesitant having only me there to defend you."

Jax smiled but kept her thoughts to herself. If the Duchy of Pettraud was a part of this plot, being around Perry alone posed a significant risk to her safety. And even if he was innocent, she'd long ago learned men were not always the brave fighters they thought they were.

Captain Solomon joined them shortly after they finished eating, ready to escort them down to the stables. As he approached the couple, he gave Jax a wink, and she wished ever so dearly she could involve George in her scheme. Keeping this secret was beginning to eat away at her.

"I don't believe we have met," the Captain said, reaching a hand out in introduction to Perry. "I am George Solomon, Captain of the Ducal Guard."

Perry took his hand and shook it with surprising scrutiny. "Lord Pettraud."

Captain Solomon eyed Perry for a critical moment, leaving Jax to wonder what his impressions of her future consort were…and why she cared so much that they got along with one another. "Shall we head to the horses?" he asked Jax after a beat.

As the trio strode through the palace halls, Perry leaned closer to Jax, his voice a whisper. "This man has been responsible for protecting you your whole life? He looks only a few years older than we do."

"Since I was nine. George enlisted when his was sixteen."

Perry's eyebrows rose to his hairline. "George?"

Jax's cheeks grew warm. Members of the royal family were usually not as close to their guardsmen as she and Captain Solomon were.

"Is this *friendship* something I should be concerned about?" Perry's question was soft, free of judgement, but he was clearly worried by the possible answer.

Jax considered her words carefully. She didn't feel like rehashing adolescent whims that had long been buried. "He's one of my oldest friends, but you, nor your father, need to worry about him."

Her response triggered Perry to stand a bit taller as they walked together, a spring in his step.

Captain Solomon led his charges outside, toward the stables, allowing Perry the chance to admire more of her estate. The stables were the home to over fifty thoroughbred horses, each more beautiful and able than the last.

Jax preferred to ride a midnight stallion named Mortimer, while Perry chose a dapple mare called Babette. The stablemaster and his men quickly tacked up the horses once selections had been made. Without assistance, Jax swung her leg over her mount, causing a few raised eyebrows that she was not riding sidesaddle. Perry bounded up onto his horse, looking completely at ease in the intricately stitched saddle.

"What a fine beast you've got there," he said with a nod to Jax's stallion.

She fondly rubbed Mortimer's mane, admiring the glistening black horse. "He was a gift from Duke Crepsta and his wife for my eighteenth birthday."

"Crepstian stallions are favored amongst many a knight. I, myself, have one in the stables back home." At the mention of his estate, Perry's expression grew reflectively somber.

"You must send for him then. We cannot have you without your favorite horse." Jax urged her mount forward toward the gates where Captain Solomon waited.

"Thank you, Jax. I will." Perry sounded genuinely touched at her request. "In the meantime, I'm sure Babette will do just fine."

As he promised, George gave them a wide berth, allowing them plenty of privacy to talk freely about growing up royal and all it entailed. Perry was particularly candid with stories about being the seventh son of a Duke, and how most days, he simply wished he could be anyone else but a useless heir. Jax, on the contrary, shared how being the only child of the great Duke Saphire had caused for much unwanted responsibility. She admitted that she often felt overwhelmed as a teenager, knowing the weight of Saphire's mantle would one day rest on her shoulders, thus why she was so desperate to escape to the Academy.

Perry had been privately tutored his entire life and found her stories about the revered university completely fascinating.

All while they chatted, Jax led their party to the tavern Master Vyanti had mentioned, and by midmorning, it came into view.

"The Blind Unicorn?" Perry chuckled, reading the sign hanging over the well-maintained building.

Jax noticed he was barely winded from the long ride. Following his gaze to the three-story inn, she noted his confusion, for the place was rather upscale for a rural watering hole.

"The owner found a wounded unicorn on this parcel of land after he purchased it from a noble family," she explained. "The poor thing had lost its eyes battling another creature. He nursed the beast back to health, and in return, it decided to stay. What better attraction than a unicorn?" Jax giggled as she told the story, remembering the times she came here as a child to see Beau. Sadly, the enchanted creature passed away four summers ago, the tavern now a memorial to the famed stallion.

"Would you believe me if I told you I've never seen a unicorn up close before?" Perry asked.

Jax whipped her head around. "Never?"

"Only in picture books." Perry sighed. "Pettraudian hunters decimated their population years before I was born. I find it one of the saddest things in our history, really."

It made Jax's heart ache to think about the annihilation of such purity. The creatures possessed a special aura that made anyone who stroked their manes incredibly happy for a time, which is why so many had been domesticated a hundred or so years ago. But the duchies got together, knowing that this false happiness was not good for their people, and banned the taming of unicorns. They were meant to be wild, her father always reminded her whenever she begged for one as a pet. The Blind Unicorn's owner was only allowed to keep Beau because the creature's magic had mysteriously disappeared with its eyes.

Captain Solomon trotted up alongside them, giving Jax a reprimanding look. "Your Grace, you know I cannot allow you to have refreshments here," he said in formality.

Jax rolled her eyes, her annoyance bubbling up. "I had the kitchen prepare a picnic, Captain. You need not worry that I'll break the rules. I simply wanted to show Lord Pettraud where the legendary blind unicorn lived." She cursed inwardly, knowing George would never allow her to go inside and ask about the royal carriage's visit. Discreetly pulling out the map Master Vyanti had marked up, she urged Mortimer forward and continued their journey.

The Saphire roads were in decent shape, an initiative she and her father had worked on nearly three years ago. Too often had she visited a duchy that failed to maintain their roads outside city limits, causing merchants to delay and lose cargo on the disheveled paths.

Having not had any rain in the past ten days, Jax's keen gaze kept watch for any disturbances along the road.

About forty minutes after they'd passed the Blind Unicorn, Jax detected something promising. A deep set of carriage tracks seemed to veer off the road, crushing a large bramble bush, leaving berries squashed all over the earth. "I think I need to stretch my legs for a bit. What do you say, Perry?" Turning in her saddle, she slid gracefully off Mortimer's sweaty back.

Perry hopped to the ground and reached for the saddlebags tied to Jax's horse. "I wouldn't mind digging into the picnic, if you're up for it?"

"I never say no to food. Why don't you set everything up over there?" She pointed to a small clearing on the opposite side of the road. "I'll join you in a moment."

Without any protests, Perry hauled their treats over to the spot she'd indicated, while Captain Solomon cautiously guarded them from the road.

"I see some flowers I want for my nightstand, Captain. I'm just going to go pick them before joining Lord Pettraud," she stated, not really asking for permission. Seeing the Captain nod in understanding, she carefully followed the carriage trail off the road, through a wall of broken bushes. The tracks stopped shortly after, only to circle back onto the road a few feet up ahead.

Glancing around, Jax examined the scene. *This must be where the assassins ambushed the envoy and ushered the horses off the road. I wonder if the guards were even able to put up a fight.* Her eyes traced the disturbed grass and dirt. With ease, she detected a myriad of footprints around the indents left by the wheels. Her insides grew cold. *My parents were dead by the time they arrived here. Whoever found them must have had a hand in their death.*

From the corner of her eye, something flapped in the wind, caught on a bush. Swiftly, she reached out, untangling a small piece of fabric from the thorny branches. Turning the material over in her fingers, she guessed the blue and red scrap was made of silk, most likely torn from a tunic. Not knowing as much about textiles as she would like, she'd have to ask the royal tailor what kind of silk it was, as there were numerous styles throughout the realm. Only then, could she begin to narrow down who and where this had come from.

Deep in thought, Jax ambled back to where her companion lay sprawled out on the grass, soaking up the invigorating sun, a glass of honeyed mead half-empty in his hand. She sat down on the blanket beside Perry, picking a grape from the basket and popping it into her mouth.

Captain Solomon appeared at the edge of the clearing, his hand grazing the sword that hung from his trim waist. "The flowers not to your liking after all, Your Grace?"

Startled, she foolishly realized she'd not followed through on her ruse. "No, they were already wilting, unfortunately," she said in a dismissive tone, something she normally refrained from using around George.

"Perhaps we shall find some on our return journey?" Perry lazily suggested, squinting his eyes up at her.

She replied by pouring herself some mead, sipping it greedily. Their picnic was spent in a comfortable silence, although Jax felt ill at ease with the dark way Captain Solomon watched her. Had he figured out her true intentions for this trip? He couldn't be involved with this plot, could he? She did her best to ignore him, and instead, busied herself with studying Perry. With the sun sparkling on his pale skin and dark ringlets of hair, he was truly a beautiful specimen. He had fallen asleep, his lips parted slightly in loose relaxation. She found herself wondering what it would be like to kiss those lips, resisting the urge to reach out and stroke his cheek.

She cursed internally at her diverted attention. Here she was, longing for physical attention when she had a piece of a traitor buried in her dress pocket. She had to get back to the palace and question her tailor at once.

"Perry, shall we return home? I have some matters to attend to before supper." Jax's request was clearly not up for debate.

Twitching as he heard her voice from his dreams, Perry pulled himself off the ground, his expression resigned. "Saphire truly is breathtaking, Your Grace," he commented reverently, and she filled with pride.

‡

Their journey home was uneventful, with the occasional stop to greet commoners and nobles traversing the roads. All were quite taken with the Duchess, who forced herself to act graceful and charming, despite her heavy heart. She hoped word would spread of how serene she appeared, clearly strong enough to lead in the wake of personal tragedy.

They arrived in the palace courtyards by midafternoon, where Jax quickly passed her horse off to a waiting stable hand. "I'll see you for dinner," she said to Perry, not even paying attention to his response as she walked briskly into the grand hallway.

As she ambled the halls alone, she regretted her erratic treatment of Perry, as she'd let her agitation get the better of her manners. She'd apologize for her abrupt mood swing when she saw him later. Tired and sweaty in her riding clothes, Jax contemplated whether to change before going to see the royal tailor, but her patience had run its course. Rushing to the southern wing of the castle, it only took her a few minutes to find his chambers.

"Monsieur Duval, may I have a word?" Jax knocked on his door, restraining herself from pounding. The scrap of fabric burned a hole in her pocket with the secrets it contained.

"Duquessa! I was not expecting you. How may I be of assistance?" The flamboyant young man scrambled to attention when he saw who was at his door.

"I am sorry to surprise you, Monsieur, but I have an important question for you." Jax rushed in, shutting the door behind her. The tailor's main quarters doubled as his workshop, various pieces of cloth and silk draped everywhere in a haphazard fashion. How the renowned palace tailor got any work done in this mess was beyond her, but the artist before her truly was gifted, despite his young age.

"But of course, Your Grace." He flourished his accented words with a bow.

Jax pulled the torn fabric from the pockets of her dress, her story carefully crafted. "I was out riding today when I came across a woman wearing the most gorgeous dress. She was far enough ahead of my riding party that I could not call out to her, but I noticed her gown snagged on a nearby bush. I picked this piece of silk from it. Could you tell me what you know about this material? I must order you some for my summer gowns."

Taking the scrap in his calloused hands, the tailor examined it profusely, as if it contained the secret to eternal life. "This is monarch silk, Duquessa. Made from the chrysalis of butterflies. Quite rare in this province."

Jax's heartbeat quickened. "Might you know where it comes from?"

The young man nodded, eager to show off his wealth of material knowledge. "This particular piece looks to have come from a lion butterfly, Duquessa. Lion butterflies are known to be found in Tandora, Crepsta, and Cetachi."

Cetachi, Jax thought bitterly. The untamed region that was also the possible source of the bloodsleaf. "Cetachi, you say? Are they civilized enough to make silk?"

Monsieur Duval pushed his tiny spectacles down his nose, his look berating her prejudice. "Duquessa, the Cetachi people may not bow to the dukedoms, but that doesn't mean they are not artists in their own right. Many a season's styles are dictated by what comes out of Cetachi. Remember the ceremonial gown you wore during your last Savant trip? That was inspired by Cetachi tailoring."

Rather than rebuke him for his tone, she accepted his lesson in humility. She did have a jaded view of the region because she knew very little about it. Perhaps that's why all this was happening. Her family had ignored Cetachi for too long. She turned away from the tailor, pinching her nose to alleviate the building pressure. Composing herself, she thanked Monsieur Duval for the information and took the fabric from his hands.

"Shall I order a ream?" he asked, somewhat taken aback by her change in mood.

"You know, the more I look at it, the more I think it doesn't compliment my skin tone." Jax flippantly held the scrap up to her cheek. "Don't you agree?"

Duval bowed low, not even glancing at her face. "Of course, Duquessa."

Sighing, she longed for the day when someone had the courage to disagree with her. Bidding the tailor farewell and leaving him to his work, Jax strolled back to her study in contemplative silence.

Chapter Nine

She half-hoped Vyanti would be sitting in a chair when she entered her private study, but she found it ominously empty. The curtains had been pulled shut, blocking the afternoon sun. A lone candle flickered beside the doorframe, waiting to ignite the other wicks in the room. Opting for sunlight over candlelight, Jax threw back the heavy fabrics blanketing the windows, and a rush of purifying warmth flooded the room. Even though it was cleaned regularly, she saw whirlwinds of dust rising as she glided over to her desk. Taking a key that hung tucked away under the neck of her dress, she unlocked the bottom drawer and placed the fabric inside, securing it from any prying eyes. After all, it was evidence in a murder investigation and needed to be kept safe.

Sitting down at her overflowing desk, Jax busied herself with paperwork to pass the time. Vyanti had warned her he may need to stay overnight in the market until the bloodsleaf merchant arrived, so she did not expect him home just yet. She needed the distraction the rolls of parchment offered to keep her mind from conjuring accusations that were based on little evidence. Sitting there in her stately seat, Jax knew she had the power to send her armies to Cetachi's borders and tear down their defenses as payback for their treachery. As soon as the idea appeared in her head, she chastised herself for jumping to irrational conclusions. She had been trained to act better than this. She would reserve further judgment until Master Vyanti returned with his report.

She joined Arnie and Perry for dinner, relying on her friends to keep the conversation flowing. She listened politely to their back and forth on the best brushes for painting a sunset, but her mind wandered throughout the meal. It was only the gentle prodding of Arnie's foot that snapped her to attention.

"Did you hear what I said, Jax?" Arnie's concern was written all over her face.

"I'm so sorry." Jax forced herself to focus. "I was thinking about a trade agreement I've been asked to ratify. What was it you were saying?"

"Earl Crepsta responded to your invitation to stay at the palace. He'll be arriving in three days." Arnie frowned at the blank look on the Duchess's face. "…if the offer still stands."

Jax needed only a moment to recall her scheme to secure an engagement for her friend. "Of course the Earl is still welcome here! I'm so glad he'll be able to come."

Arnie's smile was one of lovesick joy. "I will make all the preparations, Jax. You won't have to worry about a thing."

Stuffing the last bit of roast beef into her mouth, Jax held up a finger while she chewed. "Please make sure that you arrange a private meeting for the Earl and me the afternoon he arrives." She gave her lady-in-waiting a knowing look before setting down her silverware. "I'm afraid our ride today really took a toll on my muscles, Perry. I am going to retire early to my chambers to recover."

Wishing them both an enjoyable evening, Jax quickly shuffled her way back to her room. Her nerves were on edge, wishing she had the courage to deny Arnie this one bit of happiness, or at least postpone it. Having Perry around was strenuous enough, but hosting another foreign dignitary whilst trying to get to the bottom of her parents' murders? She prayed Vyanti would return this evening with news.

‡

She waited for the physician until midnight before drifting off to sleep, her dreams a constant barrage of ghastly images. The whole night, she fought against faceless captors, only to be thrown into a dark cage before being tossed into a raging sea. When she woke, dark circles hung from her eye sockets.

Uma had to work a bit harder during their morning routine, applying a heavy layer of powder to cover up the signs of distress. A Duchess couldn't walk around like this, looking weak.

Perry requested permission to spend the morning painting in the palace gardens, something she heartily agreed to. While his affable nature charmed her, she was in no mood to entertain him after a fitful night. However, her duties as a hostess would require her to join him for lunch.

While her guest enjoyed the bountiful sunshine, Jax remained cooped up in her study, feeling like a prisoner locked away in a tower. Her counterparts throughout the realm must have all agreed she'd been given enough time to mourn her losses, for her desk was piled high with royal summons and requests. Saphire's financial strength made it the most influential duchy in the realm, meaning her allies came to her first for aid. Beautraud wanted this, Hestes needed that…the list went on and on. *How in the Virtues would these nations survive without Saphire's assistance?* She grunted at the tedious requests as she waded through the stack.

Arnie interrupted her just as she stamped her seal on an agreement with Tandora's Duchess regarding a fish tax. "Jax, it's well past one o'clock. Might it be time to join Lord Pettraud for lunch?" She held out an overflowing basket in her hands.

The smell of cheese and cured ham hit Jax like a pendulum. "I had no idea it was so late in the day. Yes, let's head there now. I hope he doesn't think ill of me for standing him up."

Arnie snorted with laughter. "I don't think there's any possibility of that happening."

Jax cocked an eyebrow. "What in the Virtues do you mean?"

Arnie sighed elaborately, heaving her shoulders in a dramatic fashion. "That boy is already head over heels for you. You could probably tell him you murder kittens in your spare time, and he'd still be at your beck and call."

"Don't be ridiculous!" Jax giggled at Arnie's feigned exasperation. "He's simply being polite because the poor sod has been shipped off by his emotionally stunted father. I'm sure anyone who showed him the least bit of kindness would receive the same treatment I'm getting." Jax ignored her friend's eye roll. "Besides, have you heard the way he talks to me?"

"Yes." Arnie pushed the basket into her hands, nudging her forward. "He talks to you like you and I talk to each other. Like he trusts you and values you as a person, not as a figurehead. Like he cares for you." She eyed Jax suggestively. "I'll leave you both to your picnic." Backing away down the corridor, her lady-in-waiting respectfully gave the couple some privacy.

Moseying into the garden, a wave of heat assailed Jax, surprising her by how warm the spring day had become. She regretted her choice of gown. She'd so liked to have put on something with shorter, lighter sleeves and let the sun lick her seasonally pale skin.

Perry was still busy at his easel, a brush clenched in his mouth, while his hands work madly away at the canvas. Jax sat on a bench behind him and watched him work. From her perch, she could see he'd captured a stunning, life-like resemblance of the gardens. She had to admit, she was impressed, not only with his talent but with his focused concentration. It usually took Arnie days to produce a portrait, where Perry had managed to create a beautiful scene, worthy of her palace walls, in mere hours.

Her growling stomach interrupted her appreciation of the sight before her, and she demurely cleared her throat, hoping she didn't scare the master at work. If he was startled by her appearance, Perry didn't show it. Glancing over his shoulder, he simply grinned with the brush in his mouth and indicated he would join her shortly. She used the time to unpack the picnic, nibbling on bits of cheese and fruit to satisfy her hunger.

"I'm so sorry I wasn't ready to receive you, Duchess. Sometimes I just get so caught up in a scene, I hardly notice time passing," Perry mumbled his apologies as he sat down on the bench beside her, their knees barely touching.

"I know the feeling, but then again, I don't think I find my work quite as enjoyable as you do," Jax commented through a mouthful of tangy cheese.

Perry gave her a half-sided smirk. "It might feel that way sometimes, but I can tell, deep down, you truly love your role. You have the power to enact positive change, and you know it." He sounded almost smug, like he had caught her in a lie.

Perry didn't allow her to refute his claim, for he launched into rhapsodizing about the work he'd accomplished that morning. "It's amazing," he said as he bit into an apple slice, "how much you can get done when you aren't furtively looking over your shoulder, hoping someone won't catch you in the act."

"You were really *that* afraid of your father's disapproval?"

Perry laughed darkly, shaking his head. "Goodness, no. I was afraid of the physical brutality he showed me, and—more importantly—to my work. I've had so many paintings destroyed by his hand, all because he was ashamed I enjoyed the art form."

Jax reached out, placing her hand comfortingly over his. "That's terrible. I'm so sorry."

He shrugged, sending her a grateful smile. "Well, thanks to you, I am now free of that man. At least until you get tired of me and send me packing."

As his face turned to the sun caressing his handsome features, she felt a twinge in her heart. "I don't think I'll be getting tired of you, Perry."

He squeezed her hand in answer, unable to put the emotions churning in his gaze into words.

"Your Grace." Arnie's hasty arrival interrupted their private moment. "I apologize for the intrusion, but Master Vyanti has returned to the palace with news of a plague spreading through the outlying towns. He wishes to speak with you at once in your study."

Her heart jolting with renewed purpose, Jax excused herself from a mystified Perry, leaving Arnie in her wake. Her steps were quick and determined, not at all out of line for a Duchess who'd just received word of a growing plague. Barging past the guards lining the hallways, she dismissed all who were within earshot of her workspace, ensuring she was alone when she opened the door.

Master Vyanti sat by the fireplace, disheveled from his travels. He calmly sipped tea while Jax situated herself opposite him. "Please tell me your announcement about a plague was a ruse," she pleaded.

The old physician nodded slyly, setting his cup down. "Hopefully it will give the staff something else to gossip about for a bit."

Releasing her bit of fear that the plague was real, Jax leaned forward, eyes eager. "I take it you have news?"

Vyanti looked toward the fireplace, taking a deep breath. "Indeed. I met with the Cetachi merchant this morning. He confirmed that he sold bloodsleaf to a young woman two days before your parents' accident."

"A young *woman*?" Jax's nose wrinkled. She had not been expecting that. "Could he tell you more about her?"

The physician frowned. "He said she's visited him a few times in the past, always wearing a heavy cloak that obscured most of her features."

Jax pounded her armchair in frustration. "He didn't see the color of her hair, her skin…her eyes?"

Vyanti shook his head. "He said her hair was always pulled back, masked under her hood, and her eyes were always downcast.

He did note her skin was tanned, and her hands were not calloused."

Jax was about to growl in defeat when she realized what that meant. "Not calloused? Vyanti, that could indicate she's of noble birth. Not having to do a day's hard work in her life." She let her thoughts run wild with this additional information. "Perhaps one of the Saphire noble houses is tired of my family's rule and looking to usher in new blood..." Jax stroked her cheek thoughtfully. "Could this woman have purchased the plant for any other reason? What else is bloodsleaf used for?"

Vyanti stroked his wrinkled chin. "Its toxic properties prevent it from being used in any type of medicinal alchemy. I think some less desirable folks use it as a stimulant."

Jax stood up and went back to her desk, unlocking the bottom drawer to pull out the monarch silk scrap. Bringing it to Master Vyanti, she told him about the events that had transpired during her ride to the inn and the information the tailor provided.

"Only cultivated in Tandora, Crepsta, and Cetachi?" He studied the fabric by pulling out a monocle.

"Yes, and with bloodsleaf hailing from Cetachi, I was certain I'd found the connection, but now?" Jax stared helplessly into the fire. "There are no noble families in Cetachi. And to find out she's been buying this in our own market for months." She sat there, incredulous of it all. They were no closer to finding the culprit than when they began.

Vyanti suddenly looked incredibly old and weary. "What are you thinking, Your Grace?"

She was silent for a few moments before answering. "Let us have the private burial tomorrow for my parents. After, I am going to speak with Captain Solomon about what we have uncovered. I know it is risky, but we currently have no other means of getting to the bottom of this. I need to be concerned for my own safety."

Master Vyanti seemed to want to protest, but he must have

thought better of it. "Yes, I agree with your course of action. But only Captain Solomon."

"Agreed."

Chapter Ten

The Duchess stood in black at the mouth of the catacombs, watching as eight Ducal Guards carried the wrapped bodies of her parents into the flickering darkness. Vyanti and George stood beside her, the only two permitted to attend to her during this time. Arnie had been considerably hurt she wasn't allowed to stand by Jax as her godparents were laid to rest, but she understood it was an incredibly private moment for the Duchess. The burial lasted only mere minutes, but to Jax, it felt like she watched the morbid procession for hours. When the tomb was finally sealed, she let out a long-held breath, relieved it was over.

"Captain, before you return to your post, Master Vyanti and I have something we need to discuss with you," Jax said as she clutched George's arm, her gaze heavy with anxiety.

He noticed her mood immediately and ushered them into a small, secure room just up the hall from the burial chamber.

With the door firmly shut, Jax and the physician divulged their findings from the past few days.

"What were you thinking?" George's voice was controlled, but anger radiated from his broad, imposing frame. "Do you know how gravely you've risked your safety—the security of Saphire—by keeping this all to yourself?"

She did not berate him for his insubordination, for as she had told the story, she found herself feeling increasingly foolish. Her actions *had* been irresponsible and reckless. Every minute she did not share this plot with her guardsmen, she risked her life being cut short.

Rubbing the tension clearly rising in his neck, Captain Solomon requested to speak to the Duchess alone. Acquiescing, Vyanti slipped out of the room, the door snapping shut with finality.

"Jax, how could you keep this from me? Did you truly think I was involved in this?" The emotion in his voice surprised her, and she realized the Captain of the Ducal Guard was not asking the question...her friend was.

Her eyes pooled with the sorrow wracking through her chest. "I was afraid to, George. I was so afraid," was all Jax could whimper before she melted in his comforting embrace, tears streaming down her cheeks. They stood together, sharing their pain, until Jax was finally able to speak once more.

"We thought that if we involved too many people, the culprit might get wind that we'd uncovered the murder and escape. Or worse, try again."

George sighed, his face full of agony. "I don't agree with the actions you took, but I do understand your reasoning." He took a step back from her and placed a hand on her quivering arm. "May I ask what changed your mind that you could trust me?"

Jax shirked away, biting her lip. "You've had plenty of chances to kill me before now, so I can only assume you're not a part of this. I'll be honest...we've run out of leads, and I don't know what to do."

Her words hit him hard, but he maintained a stoic expression. "You need an expert opinion." It was not a question.

She fumbled for his hand and threaded her fingers between his. "I know you would never do anything to harm my family or jeopardize them in any way. I'm sorry I let fear cloud my judgment, George."

His dark eyes examined their entwined hands for a moment before he pulled away. "From what you've told me, you and Vyanti did an incredibly good job uncovering what little clues have been left." His tone was all business. "I'll take a group of my most trusted men to the scene of the ambush and see if we can find any other leads." At her shaken look, he held up a calming palm as if to halt her spiraling thoughts. "I do not plan to tell them why we are there. It will be a simple training exercise. An assessment of their skills in detection."

"What if one of them had something to do with it?" Jax whispered.

"The men I'm taking all recently returned from southern border patrol. They haven't been near the palace or the capital city for over a month. There's no way they could be involved," George assured her, looking ever the captain in command. "I'm not asking you to trust me, Jax, but know I took an oath to protect the Crown. An oath on my own life. I have never broken a promise in all the years I've known you, have I?"

Flashes of a friendship that had spanned nineteen years ricocheted through her mind. "No, you have never gone back on your word, George." She wanted to apologize again for keeping this from him but couldn't find the right words to do her shame justice.

"I'm going to double your security until we get to the bottom of this. Arnie informed me this afternoon the Earl of Crepsta will be visiting in a few days' time. Are you sure that's wise?" He scrutinized her expressive eyes, as if trying to see what she was thinking.

"I think it's best if we go on with life as if nothing is wrong. If we are lucky, the murderer still does not know we suspect foul play." Jax straightened her black dress absentmindedly. Letting her head tilt back, she stared up at the domed ceiling. "Is there anything else, Captain? I need to retire to my rooms for the rest of the day. I'm suddenly not feeling very well."

George was at her side, offering his arm in support. "Is it something serious?"

"No. I'm just overwhelmed, that's all. Nothing a sleeping draft from Vyanti won't fix. Would you have him attend to me as soon as possible?" Jax wished she could relay her desires through Uma, but her faith in the loyalty of her staff had faltered as the investigation unfolded. Her servants were still suspect, Uma included.

"Of course. I'll send him right up. I will report immediately if we find anything of note, Your Grace." Captain Solomon bowed and left the room to prepare his men for their journey.

Jax took a few moments to herself before she left the recesses of the castle, the catacombs echoing behind her. Vyanti was already in her sitting room with a steaming sleeping draft when she arrived. He watched her drink it, giving her an uncharacteristic squeeze on the shoulder before leaving.

She knew she should reach out to Arnie before crawling back into bed; she'd promised her friend they'd have lunch together, just the two of them, but she imagined Captain Solomon had already informed her lady-in-waiting that she was not to be disturbed for the remainder of the day. Vacantly, she undressed, removed her funeral clothes and jewelry, and collapsed into bed, the sleeping draft taking hold.

‡

She wasn't sure if it was the pounding on the door or Uma's voice that woke her. Blinking heavily, Jax surveyed her room, taking in the streaming sunlight from the far east windows. It was somehow dawn again.

"Your Grace, is everything all right? You've been asleep since yesterday afternoon." Uma scurried to her side, her brow furrowed with worry.

"I slept that long? I took one of Vyanti's drafts to help me get some rest," the Duchess answered groggily. "Have I missed anything? Who's that at the door?"

"Your Grace, it's Captain Solomon." His strong, yet muffled voice penetrated the heavy door as the banging subsided. "I request an audience with you."

Jax sat straight up, her attention coming into full focus. "Uma, please inform the Captain I shall meet him in my study in ten minutes. Have you laid out my clothes already?"

Uma placed a lavender silk gown at the foot of the canopy bed before scurrying over to speak with Captain Solomon through the closed door.

Jax quickly tossed on the dress without assistance and secured her jewelry, the last being the key to her desk drawer she always wore around her neck. She noticed Uma had brought a steaming breakfast tray with her, and silently thanked the Virtues her maid was so good at her job. Eating the scrambled eggs and bacon in a most un-ladylike manner, Jax waited while Uma went back to work, twisting her hair up into something elegant, but simple.

"Your Grace, are you sure everything is all right? These past few days, well, you've been..." Uma seemed to struggle with her words, trying to gracefully not step over the line of impropriety.

"Been what?" Jax quizzed through a full mouth.

"Well, been a bit odd, I guess."

Jax placed her napkin on the small side table, quickly forming the foul-tasting lie. "The duchy is going through a period of transition, Uma. Things are changing all around us, but I can assure you, I am more dedicated to Saphire than I have ever been."

Blushing, the young woman stammered. "I-I did not mean to imply that the duchy was at risk, Your Grace. I merely wanted to make sure you were doing okay, emotionally and such."

Jax's heart softened, hoping her long-time servant really did have her best interests at heart. "Thank you for your concern, dear one, but I am fine." She wanted to divulge more, to let this young woman in on all the secrets she had been hiding—to trust her. But the gnawing fear that she had been betrayed by someone inside the palace clawed at her senses. "Breakfast was wonderful. You are excused until this evening. Enjoy a day off."

Uma's brown eyes crinkled with disappointment, like she knew Jax had been on the brink of opening up to her. "Yes, Your Grace. Thank you."

It pained Jax to know her lady's maid probably thought she was being brushed aside because Uma was common-born. Jax wished she could tell Uma there was a good reason why she was keeping her distance, but decided it was best to keep her mouth shut.

As soon as Uma departed, Jax hurried through the halls to her study to meet with George. How long had he been back from examining the ambush site? Why had he let her sleep so long? Most importantly, had his men found something she'd overlooked? She cursed herself for feeling torn. Her pride wished that they hadn't discovered anything she might have missed, while her curiosity hoped they'd found something to further the investigation.

She arrived at her destination moments later, shutting the study door with a commanding snap. Captain Solomon was the only one in the room, his face firm.

"Did you find anything new, George?" She rushed to his side.

He motioned for her to sit. "Footprints. Using our tracking skills, we found five other sets of footprints around the site, besides your own."

"Five people?"

"Five men. The shape and gait of each print suggest a band of men ambushed your parents," Captain Solomon explained, his stony gaze void of the fatigue settling across his other features. "Most telling were the soles of their shoes. Each boot print hardly had any tread."

Jax drummed her fingers on her desk. "No tread? That doesn't seem very sensible for delving in the woods."

George shook his head. "No, it doesn't. Which leaves me to believe our culprits used the only type of shoe they owned: dress shoes."

Her face lost a bit of color. "Dress shoes *and* monarch silk? We must be dealing with a rebel noble house or even another ducal family."

"Might I look at the fabric scrap you found? I might recognize the pattern from a knight's garb or military uniform."

"Of course." Turning away from George, Jax covertly pulled out her key from under her neckline and unlocked the bottom drawer of the desk. "Oh no," she whispered in horror, "it's not here anymore!"

The Captain was at her side in an instant. "What? Are you sure you put it back here?"

"I am *quite* certain." Jax's voice edged to the brink of hysteria. "This is impossible. No one knows where I hide the key to that drawer, and there's no chance they could have picked the lock. It was specially designed for my grandfather by a blacksmith who made it unbreakable. To open it, someone would need the key, and I *always* have it with me."

George seized her shaking hands, his rough touch calming her down. "Jax, you must not panic. You say you always have the key with you, even when you sleep?"

Jax's eyes widened, tears threatening to fall. "I do take it off at night and put it on the vanity in my room before going to bed."

"And there's no other copy?"

Jax's reply was barely audible. "No."

George cursed as his rage got the better of him. "Virtues' sake, that means someone came into your room last night and took it, Jax. They know about the scrap of fabric, which means they know you're investigating the deaths of your parents."

She began to shiver, despite the heat bleeding in from the glass windows. "How could someone have gotten into my room, George? You doubled the guards patrolling it!" She didn't mean to sound accusatory, but her dread made her tone sharp.

His eyes darkened. "There *are* people that have security

clearance to enter your room, Duchess."

"Uma?" Her breath caught in her throat. "No, she would never do anything like this. She's been with me since I went off to the Academy."

George didn't respond, and her mind continued to blaze through the implications. Even with the mounting evidence, denial got the better of her reasoning. "She would never betray me like this. She is too loyal a servant."

"The fact you still call her a servant after nine years of service might not exactly foster a loving relationship on her end," George stated pointedly.

"What do you mean? You think she's bitter about her role here at the palace?"

"She may not feel like she owes you anything if you haven't made the effort to connect with her." Captain Solomon stood up, closing the drawer with an echoing thud. "I'm going to go speak with the guards to find out who entered your room last night. I need confirmation before I send for Uma's arrest." The harsh actions sounded wrong on his lips.

Jax shuddered. She'd been so close to sharing her secrets with Uma minutes ago.

George wrapped an arm around her shoulder. "I'll have my men escort you to the banquet hall. I want you to stay there until this is all sorted. Your safety is everything, Jax. Please just stay put."

Jax did not object as he led her out of the room. Her confidence was in shambles. How could Uma do this to her? If she had been the one who had taken the key, then she must be involved with the larger plot, possibly being the one who added bloodsleaf to her parents' traveling canteens. All the times Uma had taken care of her and looked after her…had she been bitter that Jax was not more appreciative, more endearing? How had Jax been so wrong about the loyalties of her closest servant?

She was near tears by the time she arrived in the empty

banquet hall, her assigned patrol finally leaving her side as they dissolved quietly into shadowed corners of the room to observe. She plopped in the nearest chair and stared ruefully at the untouched place settings, suspecting it was too early for Perry and Arnie to have already eaten breakfast.

The creaking of a door startled Jax, and she turned around to see a paint-splattered Perry. His white tunic was completely covered in blotches of blue, yellow, green, and red. He grinned at her sheepishly, the dried paint on his cheeks making him look like a clown. "Good morning. I bumped into Captain Solomon as I was coming in from the gardens. He said you might need some company?"

She couldn't help but laugh at his appearance. "My goodness, what trouble have you been causing so early in the morning?" Just seeing him sent a spasm of warmth through her, soothing her racing nerves.

Perry chuckled as he grabbed a sweet roll from a nearby platter and stuffed it into his mouth. "The sunrise was ethereal this morning. I had to capture it. I also thought—since I've used up so many of Arnie's paints—I'd make some new colors to replenish her palette. Turns out, your lady-in-waiting has quite the well-stocked ingredient cabinet. I practically could mix up any color with what she keeps on hand."

"*Any* color?" Jax teased, grateful for his presence by her side. With his boyish charm, she could momentarily forget about the interrogation happening floors above.

He grinned. "I am quite talented. You'd be surprised."

Jax's eyebrows rose. "You call mixing paints a talent?"

"It's a science." Perry waved his hand with a casual flick. "It's all based in alchemy."

She snorted at his cavalier reply. "So you consider yourself an alchemist?"

"Well, if you think it's so simple…what color would you get if you mixed minx flower with elder root?" Perry asked, his lavender eyes challenging her.

Jax struggled to keep the heat from her cheeks. She had no idea what he was asking. "Blue?"

The young lord snagged another biscuit and munched on it triumphantly. "Minx flower isn't even a real thing, Jax. Come on now." He teased her, wriggling his paint-covered hands in front of her face. "But in all seriousness, you have been very generous with your lady-in-waiting for her to afford such a hobby. Some of those imported herbs are expensive."

"I pay Arnie what she deserves." Those who were appointed ladies-in-waiting did not normally receive wages in other duchies, which Jax found to be insulting and wrong. Even before Jax was crowned Duchess, with all the work Arnie put in, it only made sense to pay her as one would pay a courtier. "She's been the best lady-in-waiting I could ever ask for."

"I don't doubt it. It speaks to her character that she spends her gold on paint ingredients over fancy things like dresses and jewelry and the like. I mean, I was able to make yellow out of sun blossom and honey bane, blue from bird nettle and jasmine, red from bloodsleaf and yarlsbark, green from holly bow and mince…"

Jax knocked over an empty goblet by her arm. "Did you say bloodsleaf?"

"Yes, her cabinet was well stocked with it," Perry said, clearly oblivious to the reaction his words had caused. "Tricky plant to come by. I must ask her where she found it."

Jax felt the floor drop out from underneath her as her mind plummeted into darkness. "*Arnie* bought the bloodsleaf?"

"Jax…are you all right? You look paler than porcelain." Perry rushed to her side, grabbing her shoulders to steady her.

"We need to find Captain Solomon now!" Jax exclaimed, bursting to life in his hands. She raced from the banquet hall, her assigned guards quickly following behind with a confused Perry.

"George!" Jax cried, her voice echoing through the halls. She needed the Captain to help her make sense of it all.

"Jax!" George sprinted down the staircase from the floor above her, seeming to forget all proper decorum as he rushed to his friend's rescue. When he reached her side, his disbelieving expression told her what she already knew.

"Arnie. *Arnie* was the one who betrayed me," Jax seethed, quivering at the realization her dearest, most trusted friend, was a traitor. "She betrayed her duchy."

"How did you figure it out?" George shot a questioning look as Perry joined them, still covered in paint.

"Lord Pettraud was telling me how he mixed paints this morning using Arnie's supplies. He found her stock of bloodsleaf." Jax's voice didn't sound like her own. It was cold and unemotional.

The Captain wore a mask of great sadness. "The guards confirmed she entered your chambers last night. Only Uma and Arnie are allowed access to your rooms, Jax. I'm so sorry." His dark eyes trailed off down the hall. "She's been on the clearance list since you were seven years old." The stunning betrayal laced his incredulous words.

A hot fire ripped through her chest, her heart aching in pain. Winded, Jax leaned into Perry, using his sturdy frame for support. How could Arnie do this to her? They had been best friends since childhood. They had grown up together...as sisters. How could she do this? "We've got it all wrong, George. This can't be possible. Arnie and I were both in Hestes when Mother and Father were poisoned."

Captain Solomon's shoulders grew heavy. "I sent some men to inquire with the kitchen staff about how the rations for the Duke and Duchess's trip to Mensina were prepared."

Jax clenched her fists at her side. *Why didn't I think to do that?* She cursed her naïve investigating. How could she ever have thought she was able to solve this nightmare on her own.

George motioned to two younger guards standing behind him. "The executive chef reported that while the food was prepared and sampled the morning of their departure, the water canteens had been tasted *then* left to chill in the cold cellar for several days. Specifically, since you and Arnie stopped by the palace for an impromptu luncheon before you set off for Hestes."

"Your Grace," one of the guardsmen piped up, looking incredibly uncomfortable with the news, "some of the kitchen staff said they remembered seeing Lady Aranelda in the kitchens. She said she was picking up some treats for your long journey south."

Jax remembered the brief visit. It was a cherished, bittersweet memory, the last time she'd seen her parents alive. She and Arnie had just concluded a visit to Beautraud and had decided to make a detour home before traveling onward to Hestes. Arnie had been the one to convince Jax that it would be a delightful surprise for her parents if they stopped by for lunch. Guilt shredded her very core. "We must find her, Captain. I want her brought before me," the Duchess of Saphire commanded, her voice tinged with rage and betrayal.

"I've sent men to find her, Your Grace, but it appears Aranelda left the palace early this morning. I've sent our fastest patrols to find her." Captain Solomon saluted his men, dismissing them.

"If she left on horseback, who knows if they'll be able to catch her," Perry spoke for the first time, his face grim.

"Arnie is useless on horseback," Jax mumbled, searching her memories for reasons why this had happened, how she had lost her best friend to this deadly scheme. She couldn't have been acting alone. The footprints near the ambush site were from a band of noblemen. And how did she know to look for the torn scrap of fabric...?

"Virtues." Jax had been so focused on Cetachi, so quick to pin her suspicions on the rogue nation, that she completely dismissed Monsieur Duval saying the monarch silk could have come from

Tandora or Crepsta. *Crepsta*, the homeland of Arnie's beloved Hadrian, whom she desperately wanted to marry. What better wedding gift than helping the Duke of Crepsta claim the throne of Saphire? "I know where she would have gone, George."

‡

Although she argued and threatened a night in the dungeons, Captain Solomon would not let Jax accompany his legion of men on the chase. Deep in her heart, she knew Arnie would have fled the palace to meet Hadrian at their lovers' rendezvous, an abandoned cottage on the outskirts of Creblin, an insignificant town on the border of Saphire and Crepsta. During their years at the Academy, Arnie and Hadrian frequently snuck off to the secluded spot to spend time alone together, without the watchful eyes of Duke Crepsta's spies reporting his nephew's every move. In recent years, Arnie's duties had limited her ability to visit the retreat, but Jax knew the couple still met in secret every so often.

The Duchess sat in the throne room, lit by only the sunlight filtering in through the windows. Her insides had been turned to stone, the depth of Arnie's betrayal silencing her heart like some sort of magical enchantment. Her face was streaked with silent tears, her eyes a mirror of a thousand memories. She and Arnie had been through everything together. How could the woman she loved like a sister do this to her? To them? How had a man's hand in marriage become so much more important?

She barely heard a side door click open. "Jax?" Perry's voice trembled with trepidation.

She continued to stare straight ahead, unmoving.

He climbed up the stairs of the throne's platform, his tailored boots hardly making a sound on the stone. "I remember after losing my mother, all I wanted was for someone to sit with me. Not to talk or to comfort, but just to share the same air, to know I wasn't alone.

It may seem silly, but today, I bet you feel like you lost someone."

Closing her eyes, she let his words reverberate inside her mind. He was right. She had lost someone. Someone she had treasured so greatly, an aching pain gnawed at her heart. She felt like she had lost some of herself, too...her ability to trust.

Perry finally arrived beside her and crouched next to her chair.

"How is it possible that this hurts worse than finding out my parents died?" she whispered, ashamed to share such an intimate revelation.

Perry took a deep breath, his voice soft and tender. "I suppose you knew you would eventually have to live through the passing of your parents at some point in your life. I don't think you ever expected Arnie to do something so savage as this. That might be why the betrayal hurts more." He reached out a warm hand to clasp hers, massaging it gently.

At his touch, she opened her amethyst eyes and met his gaze. He had changed into a dark green tunic and scrubbed away the paint. He sat there on the floor next to her, holding her hand, looking out across the empty throne room. She slid out of her chair and shuffled to his side on the floor, leaning into his broad chest. "Thank you for being here, Perry."

He kissed the top of her head, pulling her close. "Always, Jax."

Chapter Eleven

George sent a messenger ahead of their party to inform Jax that they would be arriving at the palace with their captives. Uma helped her wash her face and laced her into her most formidable gown, a dark green dress that was exquisitely stitched with silver flames around the hem. She was an avenging queen, having selected a black onyx crown to wear during the interrogation. Never had she felt more fearsome or powerful.

She informed Jaquobie about the investigation and that the Ducal Guard had captured Arnie along with several Crepstian rogues. She gave him credit for quickly processing the whole situation with grace, and in turn, he took her into his own private library to strategize how Saphire should deal with this treachery.

"We don't want to risk starting an outright war with Crepsta until we figure out how deep this plot goes, Your Grace," he said, stroking his pointed beard. "I suggest we send a dispatch to Duke Crepsta and inform him of what we have learned. Perhaps we will find out he knew nothing about the plot, and we can let the Duchy of Crepsta go on its merry way."

He ignored her sputtering protests and continued, "This only will happen if we treat our captives well. If the Duke finds out we roughed up his nephew, he may not care why and send his army after us."

Jax knew her advisor was right. They were in dangerous territory and had to play they hand wisely. "I'll remind Captain Solomon that these prisoners are to be treated with respect, as much as they don't deserve it. Can you organize the dispatch, please? My presence is required in the throne room."

"Of course, Your Grace." Jaquobie bowed and escorted her to the door. "You can do this, Duchess. I have faith in you," he whispered, almost inaudibly, as he closed the door, and her face warmed with surprising pride.

She found Perry pacing the length of the hall outside the throne room, obviously waiting for her to arrive. In his hand, he held a chocolate-cherry tart, which he promptly placed in her palm. "I thought you might need a little something before all hell breaks loose."

Jax looked at him wryly. "You think I'll perform that badly?"

"Virtues, that's not what I meant," Perry stammered, his face turning the color of the jelly pastry.

"I know." She shushed him with a kiss on the cheek. "Thank you. How did you know these are my favorite?"

The young lord looked down at the floor. "I see you sneak one every morning after breakfast."

She glanced at him in muted shock, embarrassed. "I didn't think anyone ever saw me do that!"

Perry met her gaze. "It's hard to notice anything else when you're in the room, Jax." He took her hand and kissed it, his eyes never breaking their connection. "Good luck in there. I'll be here for you when it's all done with."

The stone wall she'd forged to protect her heart began to crack. "Come in with me, please." Her request was barely a whisper, but her companion nodded his understanding.

☦

Sitting atop her throne, she prayed for the Virtues to give her strength. She could not risk making a scene when Arnie came through those doors. Struggling to control the surging emotions inside, Jax hoped she could keep herself in check and not disappoint Jaquobie, who stood resolutely on the steps leading up to her platform. She approached this as a true test of her ability to lead in times of chaos.

When Captain Solomon finally led his captives to the foot of her throne, she was surprised that she felt nothing. Seeing Arnie's wild hair and unkempt clothes was like looking at a stranger. No memories of their past, their childhood, flooded her mind. The woman before her was not someone she recognized.

Struggling against the grip of the guards, Arnie began screaming her name, using her title, her given name, even her nickname. But her pleas fell on deaf ears. Jax sat there, numb at the sight of the traitor. At last, she forced her gaze down on the fallen woman with grim triumph.

"Aranelda of Saphire, we have evidence proving you poisoned the late Duke and Duchess the morning they left for Mensina's tournament. We have reason to believe you did this on behalf of the Duchy of Crepsta, with the intention to either kill me or invade Saphire during this time of mourning and claim the throne for Duke Crepsta. Do you deny these claims?" Jacqueline Arienta Xavier, Duchess of Saphire, stood tall in front of her throne, looking down on the horde of conspirators.

"Claim it for my uncle?"

Jax glanced behind Arnie to see golden-haired Hadrian stepping forward.

His lip curled into a snarl. "That's what you think this is all about?"

Jax gave her full attention to the pompous Earl, raising an eyebrow. "If I have gotten it so horribly wrong, Earl Crepsta, please, enlighten my court."

"My wretched uncle would never have gotten his hands on Saphire. Aranelda and I planned to take your throne for ourselves!" Hadrian laughed maniacally.

"Why did you seek the throne?" Jax asked sharply.

"Because then my uncle would have to bow to *our* demands.

For years, he has been blocking my attempts to marry Aranelda. He said she wasn't suitable for me because she didn't come with a duchy. He wanted me to marry a Duchess, so I could rule a nation of my own." Hadrian sounded like a sniveling child. "But he never understood that we truly loved each other. I was not going to let her go." The Earl reached out and grabbed Arnie's hand, clasping it desperately. "We decided that to be rid of his meddling, I needed a Duke's power and influence, equal to his own, which meant I needed a duchy to usurp. With Arnie's connections here, our plan fell into place."

"Did you really think you'd succeed in overthrowing my rule?" Jax inquired, her tone a staunch bit disbelieving.

"We planned to assassinate you," Hadrian boasted with a flippant shrug, "and since you have not birthed an heir, we could have swooped right in. Arnie is widely known as your closest and dearest friend. Over her years of service, she has gained the respect and love of your people. They would have welcomed her with open arms, especially the noble houses of Saphire. To have one of their own in power...it would have changed the very structure of the realm. It's high time we had noble blood assume a throne."

It was Captain Solomon's turn to spit out a question. "And you think the Saphirian Ducal Guard would just let an outsider take the Crown?"

"I have been recruiting a small army, unbeknownst to my uncle. They were prepared to take your castle using force if needed." Hadrian began to strut around, clearly unhinged with delusions of grandeur.

"I've heard enough." These wild ideas exhausted the last of her patience. "Captain, I'd like you to lead a delegation to Crepsta. Take one of our court scribes to provide a transcript of this meeting bearing my seal." She glanced at the cluster of robed men in the back of the room, who had been furiously writing down every moment of the session. "I believe the Earl needs to be returned to his uncle," she said, staring coldly into Hadrian's amber eyes, which suddenly clouded with fear. "The Duke shall be held responsible for punishing this warmongering nephew of his."

"Please, let me go with him, Poppy." Arnie's plea was small and almost lost in the clamor of Hadrian and his men, but Jax heard it like a piercing shriek.

"You will address me as 'Your Grace,' should you ever have the honor of speaking to me again," Jax hissed, her fists clenched behind her back, hidden from view of the others gathered in the room. "No, Aranelda, you will remain here in Saphire, locked away for the remainder of your traitorous life."

Jaquobie cleared his throat. "Your Grace, the penalty for treason is death, should you choose." His words hung in the air like a hangman's noose.

The Duchess stared at her former lady-in-waiting for a long moment, remembering Hadrian's words, '*We planned to assassinate you.*' Words that would haunt her forever.

"I could never take the life of a friend, High Courtier." Jax descended her pedestal, taking the outstretched hand awaiting her and walked out of the throne room with Perry at her side.

Epilogue

Captain Solomon returned a mere fortnight after the prisoners' delegation departed. Duke Crepsta had been utterly appalled and shocked to learn what his nephew had done and immediately condemned Hadrian to death. George had brought back Hadrian's noble seal as proof that the man had been dealt with.

The army amassed by the Earl had been blackmailed into believing Hadrian and his cronies would murder each man's family if they refused to join in the fight, and subsequently pledged their loyalty to Duke Crepsta by enlisting in the Duke's forces. George also carried a lengthy apology from Crepsta and his wife. The note stated more than once how stunned they were to learn about this plot, and they repeatedly begged forgiveness on behalf of the nation, which Jax was quick to give. She did not hold the Duke accountable for his nephew's murderous actions.

In the days that followed the trial, Jax did not have the slightest desire to visit Arnie. Her curiosity had been satisfied as to why the woman she loved as a sister betrayed her. In the end, Arnie's love for Hadrian and lust for power overshadowed any devotion she had once had to Jax.

People do horrible things for love, she thought as she strolled in the moonlight under a garden trellis. But I can't forget people also do wonderful things for it, as well.

Perry's figure stood in the clearing before her, starlight pooling around him. Hope fluttered in her chest. Their bond grew stronger with each passing day they spent together. She knew she owed Duke Pettraud a finite answer about their engagement. Where she once felt that she would begrudgingly accept the offer, she now looked forward to the moment when she would secure her future with Perry.

Her father always wished that she'd be able to marry for love, and she had a feeling that it might just come true.

The End

Murder is a royal affair.

Look for the *Ducal Detective Mysteries* on eBook and paperback.

The Ducal Detective Mysteries
The Ducal Detective
A Feast Most Foul
A Voyage of Vengeance
A Summit in Shadow
Throne of Threats

The Court of Mystery series
Paradise Plagued
Burdened Bloodline
Sovereign Sieged
Crown of Chaos

www.saraheburr.com

Connect with Ms. Burr on Twitter (@SarahEBurr).

Acknowledgements

A hearty thanks to Evan Grant, Angelina Gennis, and Francelia Plank for lending their eyes for the editing process.

A special thank you to Mihail Uvarov; cover design by www.Ecover.pro

Dedications

To Mom and Dad for encouraging me to follow my dreams
And
To George for the past, present, and future

Made in the USA
Middletown, DE
23 April 2021